Caring for children—and captivating hearts!

The doctors and nurses of Paddington Children's Hospital are renowned for their expert care of their young patients, no matter the cost. And now facing both a heart-wrenching emergency and a dramatic fight to save their hospital, the stakes are higher than ever!

Devoted to their jobs, these talented professionals are about to discover that saving lives can often mean risking your heart...

Available now in the thrilling
Paddington Children's Hospital miniseries:

Their One Night Baby by Carol Marinelli
Forbidden to the Playboy Surgeon by Fiona Lowe

And coming soon...

Mommy, Nurse...Duchess? by Kate Hardy
Falling for the Foster Mom by Karin Baine
Healing the Sheikh's Heart by Annie O'Neil
A Life-Saving Reunion by Alison Roberts

Dear Reader,

When I was invited to be part of the Paddington Children's Hospital series, I jumped at the chance to spend some virtual time in London. Oh, what fun I had "walking" the streets virtually, online—first in Paddington and then venturing farther afield as I gave my Aussie heroine a London adventure.

My favorite part of this research was the setting for the fund-raising ball. I based it around the Savoy Hotel and the wild and wonderful stories that are now part of the folklore of that gracious establishment.

I hope you enjoy spending a few hours in London with Claire and Alistair as they work and play and finally find their happy-ever-after.

Check out my Pinterest page for the book to see some of the London sights that feature in it. Online, you can find me at fionalowe.com, on Facebook, Twitter and now Instagram, and you can email me at fiona@fionalowe.com. I love to hear from my readers.

Happy reading!

Fiona x

FORBIDDEN TO THE PLAYBOY SURGEON

FIONA LOWE

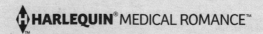
HARLEQUIN® MEDICAL ROMANCE™

Special thanks and acknowledgment are given to Fiona Lowe for her contribution to the Paddington Children's Hospital series.

Recycling programs
for this product may
not exist in your area.

ISBN-13: 978-0-373-21521-8

Forbidden to the Playboy Surgeon

First North American Publication 2017

Copyright © 2017 by Harlequin Books S.A.

Printed in U.S.A.

www.Harlequin.com

Books by Fiona Lowe

Harlequin Medical Romance

Sydney Harbor Hospital: Tom's Redemption
Letting Go with Dr. Rodriguez
Newborn Baby For Christmas
Gold Coast Angels: Bundle of Trouble
Unlocking Her Surgeon's Heart
A Daddy for Baby Zoe?

Visit the Author Profile page
at Harlequin.com for more titles.

To my fellow Medical Romance author
Annie O'Neil, who answered all my questions
about London so enthusiastically and speedily.
And for the laughs. Thanks! It made writing this
book so much fun.

CHAPTER ONE

Although Claire Mitchell had been in London for a few weeks, she still pinched herself every time she stepped out onto the streets of Paddington. For an Aussie country girl, it was all a little bit surreal—like being on the set of *Mary Poppins* or *Upstairs, Downstairs*.

Dazzling white, Victorian, stuccoed terraced houses with pillared porches and decorative balconies were built neatly around tiny central gardens. This morning as she crossed the pocket-handkerchief park, passing between two black wrought-iron gates, the ubiquitous London drizzle was cheerfully absent. Tongues of early-morning light filtered down between the tender, bright green spring foliage of century-old oaks and elms. It was a far cry from the dusty, rock-hard and sun-cracked park where she'd spent her childhood. The only shade to be found at the Gundiwindi playground had been that cast by the people standing next to her.

Walking briskly, she made her way along what would be a frantically busy road in an hour's time. Right now though, the street sweepers, bakers, newsagents and baristas were the only people out offering services to a few crazy early birds like herself. Her favourite Italian trattoria had a coffee window and Tony greeted her with a cheery *buongiorno* as he handed out six lattes, neatly stacked in a cardboard carrier. 'You bring the sunshine, *mia bella.*'

Claire smiled and gave into the irrational zip of delight she allowed herself to feel. She knew the garrulous barista flirted with every female aged two to ninety-two and that his *mia bella* meant nothing. But as few men ever noticed her, let alone tried to charm her, she accepted and enjoyed his compliments as a lovely way to start her day.

She bought a *pain au chocolat* from the bakery and balanced the bag on top of the coffees as she continued to walk towards Paddington Children's Hospital, or 'the castle' as the locals called it. A bright red double-decker bus lumbered past down the narrow road. With her free hand, she grabbed a quick photo of it on her phone and immediately sent it to her brother. He was the proud owner of the Gundiwindi garage and he adored anything with an engine. Whenever Claire saw something he'd delight in, she always sent him a photo. He always replied with either a picture of her nieces and nephews or of her parents.

Unlike herself, David loved living in the small outback town where they'd both grown up. Good at both cricket and footy, he'd always belonged and thrived and he couldn't imagine living anywhere else. She, on the other hand, had been plotting to leave since she was ten years old, desperate to escape the taunts and bullying of a small-minded town that hovered on the edge of the desert and existence.

The imposing turrets of the red-brick London hospital now loomed high above her as she approached the old ornate gates. A small group of people rugged up against the post-dawn chill clutched *Save Our Hospital* and *Kids' Health NOT Wealth* signs with gloved hands. Each morning found a different combination of people in attendance. Many were parents of current patients, but hearteningly, there were some who'd been patients themselves many years ago. Together they were united and maintained a peaceful protest presence at the gates, striving to keep alive the hope that something could be done to save the hospital from closure.

'I've brought hot coffee,' Claire called out, holding up the cardboard tray as she did most mornings. Granted, she'd only been working at the castle for a few weeks but the idea of central

London losing such a vitally important health-care provider was a terrifying thought. What if the castle had already been closed when West-bourne Primary School caught fire? The thought made her shudder. There would have certainly been deaths. Even with the hospital's proximity to the school, there'd been far too many close calls. Not everyone was out of the woods yet, includ-ing little Ryan Walker.

The stalwarts at the gate greeted her and her coffees with a cheer. 'Morning, love.'

'Early again? You still on Aussie time?' one asked.

She laughed. 'I'd be going home after a day's work if I was.'

Once she'd distributed the coffees, she ducked through the gates and strode under the decorative brick archway. Behind the beautiful Victorian façade was a modern hospital with state-of-the-art equipment and an experienced and dedicated staff. There were one hundred and fifty years of history here and she was humbled to be a part of it. When she'd received the offer of a chance to train under the tutelage of the world-renowned neurosurgeon, Alistair North, she'd actually squealed in delight, deafening the very proper Englishwoman on the other end of the line.

'Now, now, Ms Mitchell,' the secretary to the chair of the Royal College of Surgeons had said

primly as if overt displays of enthusiasm were
frowned upon. Then, without pausing, she'd continued to outline the terms and conditions of the
scholarship.

Claire hadn't cared about her unrestrained
antipodean response. If a girl couldn't get excited
about such an amazing opportunity, when could
she? After all, her work was her life and her life
was her work, and the scholarship was a chance
of a lifetime. At the time, she'd danced down the
corridors of Flinders Medical Centre telling everyone from cleaners to consultants that she was
going to London.

Now, as she ran up five flights of stairs, she
was almost certain that if she'd known what was
in store for her at the castle, she might not have
been quite so excited. When she reached the landing with the large painted koala on the ward door,
she smiled. Why, when all the other wards were
named after northern hemisphere birds and ani-
mals, the Brits had chosen an Aussie marsupial
for the neurology ward's logo was a mystery to
her but she loved that they had. It made her feel
a little less like an alien in what was proving to
be a very unexpected foreign land.

Despite speaking English and having been
raised in a country where the Union Jack still
sat in the corner of the flag, Londoners were different. The brilliant Alistair North was extremely

different, although not in the often restrained and polite British way. She'd been fortunate to work with talented neurosurgeons in Australia and she understood that brilliance was often accompanied by quirks. But Mr North had taken quirk and magnified it by the power of ten. All of it left her struggling to convince herself she'd done the right thing in accepting the scholarship.

Stepping into the bright and cheery ward, she noticed with a start that the nurses' station was empty. Surely she wasn't late? Her mouth dried as she spun around to check the large wall clock. The bright, red and yellow clock hands pointed to big blue numbers and they instantly reassured her. She gave a little laugh that contained both relief and irony. Of course she wasn't late—she was never late and today she was even earlier than usual. Preparation and attention to detail was as much a part of her as breathing. It had been that way since the fateful day in grade five when her small childhood world had suddenly turned on her.

Assuming the nurses to be busy with their end-of-shift tasks, she slid into an office chair and logged on to the computer. She always read her patients' overnight reports before rounds. It was better to take the extra time, learn what had happened and to have a well thought out plan than to be caught short. Just the thought of being put on the spot with the critical eyes of the medical students and junior house officers fixed upon her made her breath come faster.

The ward cared for children with a variety of neurological, craniofacial and central nervous system disorders, including those that required surgery. Although Mr North performed many different operations, his passion was the surgical treatment of focal epilepsy. It was the reason she'd fought so hard to win the scholarship and work with him, but as her brother often said in his laconic and understated tone after everything had gone pear-shaped, 'It seemed like a good idea at the time.' Right now she was second-guessing her good idea.

While she read the reports, the daytime nursing staff drifted in, busy chatting, and the medical students soon followed. Finally, the consistently late junior house officer, Andrew Bailey, arrived breathless and with his white coattails flapping. He came to a sudden halt and glanced around, his expression stunned. 'I still beat him?'

Claire, who'd just read little Ryan Walker's 'no change' report, stood with a sigh. 'You still beat him.'

He grinned. 'I must tell my father that my inability to be on time makes me a natural neurosurgeon.'

'Perhaps that's my problem,' Claire muttered as

she checked her phone for a message or a missed call from the exuberantly talented consultant surgeon who had no concept of time or workplace protocol. Nope, no messages or voicemail. She automatically checked the admissions board, but if Mr Alistair North were running late because of an emergency admission, she'd have been the one hauled out of bed to deal with it.

'I heard while you and I were slaving away here last night, he was holding court over at the Frog and Peach,' Andrew said with a conspiratorial yet reverent tone.

'That doesn't automatically mean he had a late night.'

Andrew's black brows rose and waggled at her. 'I just met the delectable Islay Kennedy on the back stairs wearing yesterday's clothes. She mentioned dancing on tables, followed by an illicit boat ride on the Serpentine and then bacon and eggs at the Worker's Café watching the dawn break over the Thames. When I see him, I plan to genuflect in his direction.'

A flash of anger swept through Claire's body so hot and fast she thought it might lift her head from her neck. *I want to kill Alistair North.* Surgery was such a boys' club and neurosurgery even more so. For years she'd gone into battle time and time again on the basis of raw talent but it was never enough. She constantly fought sexism, and now, it seemed, she had to tackle ridiculous childish behaviour and the adoration of men, who in essence were little boys. Fed up and furious, she did something she rarely did: she shot the messenger.

'Andrew, don't even think that behaviour like that is commendable. It's juvenile and utterly irresponsible. If you *ever* pull a stunt like that and turn up to operate with me, I'll fail you.'

Before her stunned junior house officer could reply, the eardrum-piercing sound of party blowers rent the air. Everyone turned towards the raucous sound. A tall man with thick, rumpled dark blond hair and wearing fake black horn-rimmed glasses—complete with a large fake bulbous nose and moustache—was marching along the ward with a little girl clinging to his back like a monkey. Behind him followed a trail of children aged between two and twelve. Some were walking, others were being pushed in wheelchairs by the nurses and many wore bandages on their heads—all of them were enthusiastically puffing air into party blowers and looking like they were on a New Year's Day parade.

'Wave to Dr Mitchell,' the man instructed the little girl on his back. 'Did you know she's really a kangaroo?'

Despite his voice being slightly muffled by the fake moustache, it was without doubt the unmistakably deep and well-modulated tones of Alistair North.

A line of tension ran down Claire's spine with the speed and crack of lightning before radiating outwards into every single cell. It was the same tension that invaded her every time Alistair North spoke to her. The same tension that filled her whenever she thought about him. It was a barely leashed dislike and it hummed inside her along with something else she didn't dare name. She refused point-blank to contemplate that it might be attraction. The entire female staff of the castle might think the man was sex on a stick, but not her.

Granted, the first time she'd seen all six feet of him striding confidently towards her, she'd been struck by his presence. Unlike herself, not one single atom of the many that made up Alistair North hinted at doubt. The man positively radiated self-assurance from the square set of his shoulders to his brogue-clad feet. He wore clothes with effortless ease, their expensive cut and style fitting him flawlessly, yet at the same time finding the perfect pitch between stuffy and scruffy. Despite his posh accent, there was also something engaging and decidedly un-British about his lopsided and cheeky grin. It wasn't a smile one associated with a consultant. It would break over the stark planes of his cheeks, vanquishing the esteemed surgeon and give rise to the remnants of a cheeky and mischievous little boy. But it wasn't so much the smile that undid her—it was the glint in his slate-grey eyes. He had the ability to focus his attention on a person and make them feel as if they were the only human being on the planet.

'Welcome to the castle, Mitchell,' he'd said to her on her first day.

As she'd shaken his outstretched hand and felt his firm pressure wrap around her fingers and travel up her arm, she'd been horrificd to feel herself just a little bit breathless. Her planned speech had vanished and she'd found herself replying in her broadest Australian accent, 'Thanks. It's great to be here.'

It had taken less than a week for her to realise that Alistair North's cheeky grin almost always flagged that he was about to break the rules and wreak havoc on a grand scale. She'd also learned that his eyes alone, with their dancing smoky hue and intense gaze that made the person in their sights feel like they mattered to him like no one else, were frequently used with devastating ease to tempt women into his bed.

She conceded that, perhaps, on her first day when she'd felt momentarily breathless, she'd succumbed to the hypnotic effect of his gaze. Now, after working closely with him for weeks, she was

immune to its effects. She'd spent ten years slog-
ging her way up the medical career ladder, spending more hours in hospitals than out of them, and
she wasn't about to risk it all by landing up in
the boss's bed. More importantly, she didn't like
Alistair North, so even if he were the last man
on earth, she wouldn't be tempted.

Apparently, she was virtually the only woman
at the castle with that thought. Over the past few
weeks she'd been stunned to find herself sought
out by hopeful women seeking information about
Alistair North's proclivities, or worse still, being
asked to act as go-between for disappointed and
sometimes furious women whom he'd dated and
then hadn't bothered to call. All things considered, from his casual disregard of the rules to his
blasé treatment of women, there was no way on
God's green earth or in the fiery depths of hell
that she was attracted to *that man*. Not now. Not
never.

The stories about Alistair North that circu-
lated around the hospital held fable qualities. If
she hadn't been working closely with him as his
speciality registrar, she'd have laughed on being
told the tales. She'd have said, 'They've got to be
the invention of an overactive imagination.' But
she did work with him. Sadly, she'd seen enough
evidence to know at least two of the stories she'd
heard were true so she had no reason not to be-

lieve the others. As hard as she tried to focus
solely on Alistair North's immense skill as a neurosurgeon and block out the excited noise that
seemed to permanently spin and jangle around
him, it was impossible.

Everywhere she turned, people talked about
his exploits in and out of the operating theatre.
Gossip about who he was currently dating or
dumping and who he'd been seen with driving
into work that morning ran rife along the hospital corridors. It was as if speculation about the
man was the hospital's secondary power supply.
What she hated most of all was the legendary
status the young male house officers gave him,
while she was the one left trailing behind, picking up the pieces.

No, the sensation she got every time she was in
the same space as Mr Alistair North was antagonism. The man may be brilliant and talented in
the operating theatre but outside of it he was utterly unprofessional. He was stuck permanently in
adolescence, and at thirty-nine that was not only
ridiculous, it was sad. Most of his contemporaries
were married with children but she supposed it
would take a brave—or more likely deluded—
woman to risk all on him. The only thing Claire
would risk on Alistair North was her brain. Despite what she thought of the man, she couldn't

deny the doctor was the best neurosurgeon in the country.

The little girl on Alistair North's back was now waving enthusiastically at her. Claire blinked behind her glasses, suddenly realising it was Lacey—the little girl they were operating on in an hour's time. Why wasn't she tucked up in her bed quiet and calm?

'Wave back, Kanga,' Alistair North said, his clear and precise Oxford accent teasing her. 'It won't break your arm.'

Claire's blood heated to boiling point. Did the man know that kangaroos boxed? The thought of bopping him on his fake nose was far too tempting. She felt the expectant gaze of the ward staff fixed firmly on her and suddenly she was thrown back in time. She was in Gundiwindi, standing in front of the class, with fifteen sets of eyes boring into her. She could see the red dust motes dancing in the starkly bright and uncompromising summer sunshine and the strained smile of her teacher slipping as his mouth turned down into a resigned and grumpy line. She could hear the shuffling and coughing of her peers—the sound that always preceded the one or two brutal comments that managed to escape from their mouths before Mr Phillips regained control.

Moron. Idiot.

Stop it. She hauled her mind back to the present, reminding herself sternly that she wasn't either of those things. She'd spent two decades proving it. She was a woman in a difficult and male dominated speciality and she was eleven months away from sitting her final neurosurgery exams. She'd fought prejudice and sexism to get this far and she'd fought herself. She refused to allow anyone to make her feel diminished and she sure as hell wasn't going to accept an order to wave from a man who needed to grow up. She would, however, do what she always did—she'd restore order.

In heels, Claire came close to matching Alistair North's height, and although her preference had always been to wear ballet flats, she'd taken herself shoe shopping at the end of her first week of working with him. The added inches said, *Don't mess with me*. She took a few steps forward until she was standing side on to him but facing Lacey. Ignoring Alistair North completely, and most definitely ignoring his scent of freshly laundered cotton with a piquant of sunshine that made her unexpectedly homesick, she opened her arms out wide towards the waving child.

'Do you want to come for a hop with Kanga?'

'Yes, please.'

Lacey, a ward of the state, transferred almost too easily into her arms, snuggling in against her chest and chanting, 'Boing, boing, boing.'

Claire pulled her white coat over her charge, creating a makeshift pouch, and then she turned her back on Alistair North. She strode quickly down the ward carrying an overexcited Lacey back to her bed. As she lowered her down and tried to tuck her under the blankets, the little girl bounced on the mattress.

Thanks for nothing, Alistair, Claire muttered to herself. It was going to take twice as long as normal to do all the routine preoperative checks. Yet another day would run late before it had even started.

CHAPTER TWO

ALASTAIR NORTH MOVED his lower jaw sideways and then back again behind his surgical mask, mulling over the conundrum that was his incredibly perfectionist and frustratingly annoying speciality registrar. She'd more than competently created a skin pouch to hold the vagus nerve stimulator she was inserting into Lacey Clarke. Now she was delicately wrapping the wire around the left vagus nerve and hopefully its presence would effectively minimise Lacey's seizures in a way medication had so far failed to achieve.

A bit of electricity, he mused, could kill or save a life. He knew all about that. Too much or too little of the stuff left a man dead for a very long time. What he didn't know was why Claire Mitchell was permanently strung so tight a tune could be plucked on her tendons.

Based on her skills and glowing references from the Royal Prince Alfred Hospital in Sydney and the Flinders Medical Centre in Adelaide, she'd outranked twenty-five other talented applicants from the Commonwealth. With her small steady hands and deft strokes, she had the best clinical skills of all the trainees who'd applied to work with him. She'd beaten twenty-four men to win the scholarship and that alone should tell her she was the best. Surely she knew that?

Does she though?

In his speciality, he was used to fielding egos the size of Scotland. It wasn't that Claire didn't have an ego; she did. She knew her stuff and he'd seen her run through medical students and her junior house officer with a complete lack of sympathy for any whose insufficient preparedness caused them to give incorrect answers to her questions. But he was used to trainees of her calibre thinking of themselves as 'cock of the walk' and carrying themselves with an accompanying swagger.

Claire Mitchell didn't swagger, despite the fact she had the best set of legs he'd seen on a woman in a very long time. And her shoes. Good God! Her acerbic personality was at odds with those shoes. Did she have any idea how her body moved in those heels? Her breasts tilted up, her hips swung and her calves said coquettishly, *Caress me. I promise you there's even better ahead.*

Hell's bells. He had a love-hate relationship with those shoes and her legs. Did they hint at a deeply buried wild side? Would those legs party the way he loved to party? Would he even want to party with them? *No way.* Gorgeous legs weren't enough to overcome a major personality flaw. Claire had a gritty aura of steely determination and no sense of humour whatsoever.

Given what she'd achieved so far and the fact she had a ninety-nine per cent chance of passing her exams on the first attempt—an uncommon feat in neurosurgery—she should be enjoying her hard-earned position. He doubted she was enjoying anything. The bloody woman never looked happy and it drove him crazy.

As her boss, his duty of care extended only so far as making sure she was coping with the workload and her study for her fellowship exams. However, he'd spent two years living in Australia himself, and despite both countries speaking English, pretty much everything else was different. It had taken him a few months to find his feet at the Children's Hospital and get established in a social set so he was very aware that Claire Mitchell might flounder at first. Ten days after she'd started working with him, he'd found her looking extremely downcast with what he'd assumed was a dose of homesickness. The woman looked like she needed to get out of the hospital for a bit and catch her breath.

On the spur of the moment, he'd asked, 'Would you like to grab a pint at the Frog and Peach?'

Her response had been unexpected. Her eyes—a fascinating combination of both light and dark brown that reminded him of his favourite caramel swirl chocolate bar—had widened momentarily before suddenly narrowing into critical slits. In her distinctive diphthong-riddled accent—one he really didn't want to admit to enjoying—she'd said briskly and succinctly, 'I have reports.'

'There's always going to be reports to write,' he'd said with a smile that invariably softened the sternest of wills.

'Especially when *you* don't appear to write many.'

He wasn't sure who'd been more taken aback—him, because registrars knew better then to ever speak to their consultant like that, or her, because she'd actually spoken her thoughts out loud.

'I'm sorry. That was out of order,' she'd said quickly, although not in a particularly ingratiating tone. 'Please accept my apology.'

'Jet lag still bothering you?' he'd offered by way of an olive branch. After all, they had to work together and life was easier if he got along with his trainee. So far, her standoffish manner wasn't a good sign.

At his question, a momentary look of confusion had crossed her face before disappearing under her hairline. 'Jet lag's a bastard.'

It was, but they both knew right then and there she wasn't suffering from it. She'd spent that Friday night writing reports and he'd gone to the pub determined to forget about shoes that teased and long, strong and sexy legs. Legs that should come with a warning: Toxic If Touched. Happily, he'd met a pretty midwife with a delectable Irish lilt. The music had been so loud she'd had to lean in and speak directly into his ear. Heaven help him but he was a sucker for a woman with an accent.

Claire Mitchell now snipped the last stitch and said, 'Thanks, everyone,' before stepping back from the operating table.

Alistair thought drily that after working with her over the last few weeks, he no longer had to work very hard at resisting her outback drawl. In the weeks since she'd rejected his invitation, he hadn't issued another. As long as she did her job, he overrode his concerns that she might be lonely. Of more concern to him was why he'd been working so jolly hard at trying to get her to lighten up. Hell, right now he'd take it for the win if she looked even slightly happier than if her dog had just died.

After a brief conversation with his scrub nurse, checking how her son had fared in his school athletics competition, he left Lacey in the excellent care of the paediatric anaesthetist, Rupert Emmerson. He found Claire at the computer in the staff lounge.

'That went well,' he said, pressing a coffee pod into the machine.

She pushed her tortoiseshell glasses up her nose. 'It did.'

'You sound surprised.'

She pursed her lips and her bottom lip protruded slightly—soft, plump and enticing. His gaze stalled momentarily and he wondered how it was that he'd never noticed her very kissable mouth before.

'I'm not used to children being so hyped up before surgery,' she said crisply.

And there it was—her critical tone. *That* was why he'd never noticed her lips. Her mouth was usually speaking spikey, jagged words that could never be associated with luscious, soft pink lips. He wasn't used to being questioned by staff, let alone by a trainee who was here to learn from him. If he chose, he could make her life incredibly difficult and impact on her career, but he'd learned very abruptly that life was too short to hold grudges. As far as he was concerned, in the grand scheme of things, six months was a blip on the radar.

What baffled him though was that she obviously hadn't clashed with her previous supervising neurosurgeons or she wouldn't have got this far. He struggled to align the woman at the castle with the glowing reports that had preceded her. David Wu, a surgeon of very few words, had positively gushed about the woman, calling her intuitive, skilful and courageous. It had been his recommendation that had swayed the board to offer Claire Mitchell the scholarship.

Alistair couldn't fault her surgery but he was struggling with her personality. Take this morning, for instance. Everyone on the ward had been having fun except for Mitchell, who'd looked like a disapproving schoolmistress complete with her sun-kissed blonde hair coiled into a tight knot. Like so many of his nonmedical decisions, it had been a spur of the moment thing to call out to her to wave. The moment the words had left his mouth he knew he'd done the wrong thing. It had put her on the spot and focused attention on her. He was learning that she wasn't the type of person who welcomed the spotlight.

In his defence, he'd only asked her to join in the fun because he'd found their little patient in bed, scared and trembling. He'd scooped her into his arms hoping to reassure her, and then to take her mind off things, they'd room hopped, visiting the other kids. The parade had just happened—a combination of kids being kids, some hero worship, a packet of squeakers and a little girl needing some TLC. Now Claire Mitchell had the audacity to judge it. Judge him.

'Hyped up?' he repeated, feeling the edges of his calm fraying like linen. 'Actually, I'd call it being the opposite of terrified. Lacey's spent a week being prodded and poked. She's had an MRI and a CT scan. Hell, she was attached to the EEG for two days while we recorded epileptic events so we knew which surgery to perform.'

Despite being known around the castle for his calm and relaxed approach, his voice had developed a plummy and patronising edge. 'And after enduring all of that, you'd deny Lacey a bit of fun?'

Claire's eyes flashed golden brown. 'Of course not. I'd just plan a more appropriate time for the fun.'

Her tone vibrated with her absolute conviction that her way was the right way. The only way. He remembered how once he'd been a man of absolutes and certainties and how he'd never countenanced anything ever getting in the way of what he wanted. And hadn't fate laughed itself silly over that naïve belief? Hell, it was still chuckling.

With more force than necessary, he pulled his now full coffee mug out from under the machine. Pale brown liquid spilled down the steep white sides leaving a muddy residue. 'There's a lot to be said for spontaneity, Claire.'

Her eyes dilated as if he'd just shocked her by using her first name. 'We'll have to agree to disagree on that, Mr—' She quickly corrected herself. 'Alistair.'

Good God. Frustration brought his hands up, tearing through his hair. He'd been telling her from day one to call him 'Alistair.' She'd never called him 'sir'—probably the anti-establishment Australian in her prevented her from doing that— but she'd stuck with 'Mr North.' Every time she called him by his title he responded by calling her by her surname to drive home the point. He knew it was childish and very public school, but even so, she still didn't seem to be getting the message.

He really didn't understand her at all. Hell, he couldn't even get a read on her. Every other Australian he'd ever met or worked with tended to be laid-back, easy-going and with a well-developed sense of the ridiculous. When he was a kid, he'd grown up listening to his great-grandfather recounting the antics of the ANZACs during the Second World War—brave men who didn't hesitate to break the rules if they thought any rule was stupid. What in heaven's name had he done in a previous life to be lumbered with the only dour and highly strung Aussie in existence?

'Would you like to insert the ventricular peritoneal shunt in Bodhi Singh?' he asked, returning his thoughts to work, which was a lot more straightforward than the enigma that was Claire Mitchell.

'Really?' she asked, scrutinising him closely as if she didn't quite believe his offer.

That rankled. How was it that the woman who normally couldn't detect a joke now misread a genuine offer? 'Absolutely.'

Her mouth suddenly curved upwards as wonder and anticipation carved a dimple into her left cheek.

So that's what it takes to make her smile. For weeks, he'd been trying all the wrong things.

'Thanks,' she said enthusiastically. 'I'd love the opportunity.'

The tightness that was so much a part of her faded away under the brilliance of a smile so wide it encompassed her entire face. Along with her tension, all her sharp angles disappeared too, softened by the movement of her cheeks and the dazzling sparkle in her eyes. It was like looking at a completely different person—someone whose enthusiasm was so infectious that everyone vied to be on her team.

Pick me! Pick me!

What the hell? This was worse than a momentary thought about her gorgeous legs. Utterly discombobulated, he dragged his gaze away from her pink-cheeked face that danced with excitement, and far, far away from that come-hither dimple that had his blood pumping faster than necessary. He'd spent weeks trying to make her smile, and now that he had, he knew he must make it stop. It was one thing to wish that for the good of the patients and workplace harmony his speciality registrar be a little more relaxed. It was another thing entirely to find himself attracted to her as a woman. Hell, he didn't even like her. Not. At. All.

He'd never been attracted to someone he didn't like before, but that conundrum aside, there were many reasons why any sort of attraction was utterly out of the question. First and foremost, nothing could happen between them because he was her boss and she was his trainee. Fortunately, he knew exactly how to quash any remaining eddies of unwanted desire and kill off all temptation without any pain or suffering to himself.

'Good,' he said to her, tossing the dregs of his coffee into the sink. 'I'm glad you're on board, because I promised to have lunch with the new and very attractive burns-unit house officer. Inserting the VP would make me late.'

Her tension rode back in as fast as the cavalry into battle and her eyes flashed so brightly he needed sunglasses to deflect the glare. 'You're having lunch instead of operating?'

He gave a practised shrug—one that said, *What*

of it? 'I've got complete confidence in your ability, but please, do page me if you need me.'

'I wouldn't dream of interrupting you,' she snapped.

Her previous lush mouth was now a thin, hard line and Alistair was thankfully back in familiar territory. Nothing about this Claire Mitchell was remotely attractive and his body reacted accordingly, which was to say, it didn't react at all. 'Excellent,' he said, as much to himself as to her. 'I'm glad we've got that sorted.'

Without another word, he left the room and strode towards the lifts. He'd spend the unexpected extra time with Ryan Walker's parents. It was the least he could do.

A few days later, Claire was handing out her morning coffees to the dawn crusaders at the hospital gates when she got chatting with a delightful man in his seventies. With his Cockney accent that reminded her of Eliza Doolittle's father in *Pygmalion*, he told her he'd been born 'a blue baby.'

'Me 'art's plumbing was all wrong like. Lucky for me, the castle 'ere had a pioneer in 'art surgery, otherwise I'd 'ave been dead a long time now.' Reg flicked his thumb towards the original ornate building. 'I've got a lot of love for the old girl. She gave me a chance to 'ave a bloody good life. One of me kids was born 'ere when she come early and the docs patched up the others when they broke bones. Me grandkids were all born 'ere and me first great-grandkiddy's due on Guy Fawkes.'

'It sounds like the castle is your family's hospital,' Claire said, thinking about the affection in the man's voice.

He nodded enthusiastically. 'Too right. That's why I'm 'ere every mornin'. All us Landsburys are on the rota right down to the little tackers. If that lot in suits close 'er down, it'll be a bloody disgrace.'

Claire was about to agree when she heard her name being called. She excused herself and turned to see Victoria Christie, the petite and dark-haired paramedic who'd galvanised everyone into action by starting the Save Our Hospital committee. With rapid flicks of her fingers, Victoria was motioning her over.

Bidding Reg goodbye, Claire crossed the cobblestones with care, regretting her heels. She reminded herself that her extra height would be necessary soon enough when she did rounds with Alistair. 'G'day, Vicki.'

'Hello, Claire. How are things?'

It was a broad question that really didn't demand a truthful answer but Claire had an unexpected and utterly disturbing urge to confide in the woman about how hard she was finding working with Alistair North. The thought unsettled her. She'd never been a woman who had a lot of girlfriends, and truth be told she usually got along better with men than women—which was fortunate given she was working in a male-dominated speciality. But it was immensely competitive so any friendships that had formed were always constrained by that reality.

She'd tried friendships outside of medicine but people didn't understand the crazy hours. Her frequent failures to turn up at events due to being delayed at work frustrated them and she noticed that it didn't take long for the invitations to dry up altogether. It killed relationships too, or at least it had played a big part in her and Michael's demise.

There was more to it than just your job.

She pulled her mind fast away from difficult thoughts and concentrated instead on trying to work out why women had to run in a pack and share the most intimate details of their lives with each other. She did have two close girlfriends and she'd always considered them enough, but Emma and Jessica were in Australia juggling toddlers, babies, partners and a burgeoning women's health clinic. She missed them, and these last few weeks at the castle had thrown her for a loop. Never before had she felt so at sea in a job and she had no one to talk to about her baffling boss.

How could one man generate such disparate feelings? She lurched from admiration to antipathy and back again, although right now admiration was fast losing its gloss. In Australia, she'd worked under crusty old neurosurgeons who barely knew her name and when they did deign speak to her it was to bark out instructions. It hadn't always been a pleasant experience but at least it was predictable behaviour. They'd played by the archaic rules set down a hundred years ago and she'd just put her head down and got on with the job. So why was she struggling to do that with Alistair North?

Because he doesn't play by the rules.

And wasn't that the truth! The man drove her to the point of distraction with his lack of attention to detail outside of theatre. Sure, she was his trainee, but along with her clinical work she was carrying his administrative load as well as her own and it was wearing her down. She'd been working ridiculously long hours trying to manage the paperwork and she didn't know how much longer she could trade sleep to keep up. Last week, with an enormous sense of guilt, she'd offloaded some of it onto her house officer. Andrew had accepted it without question, because that was the system, but part of her had wanted to explain. The rest of her had overruled the idea. Since leaving Gundiwindi, she'd held her secret close so it couldn't be used against her. She'd got this far and as soon as she qualified she'd be home free.

Meanwhile, she was barely treading water with the added report load, and combined with her own exhaustion and the Pied Piper incident on the ward two days ago, she'd lost her temper. Oh, how she regretted that she'd given in to fatigue and frustration. It had been beyond unwise but what worried her even more was her current pattern of behaviour. For some reason, when she was in Alistair North's company, she lost her protective restraint.

Not once in her career had she ever spoken back to her consultant, and now with the end of her fellowship in sight, it wasn't the time to start. But as each day passed, she felt more and more like a smoking and steaming volcano ready to blow. To try and keep herself in check, she'd started clenching her fists when she felt her frustrations rising. As a result, her palms had developed permanent dents in them. She'd discovered if she focused on the sharp digging pain she was less likely to say something she'd regret. It didn't always work and she'd clearly seen his displeasure at her criticism of his approach with Lacey. But instead of disciplining her, he'd rewarded her by letting her operate.

This unexpected offer had both stunned and

thrilled her. At the time, she'd hoped it meant she'd finally passed his test of attempting to drown her under a sea of administrative work. That his offer for her to operate solo meant he'd finally recognised her clinical skills and they were entering the next phase in their working relationship. For a few delicious moments she'd floated on air and then reality had hit. His offer for her to operate had been pure expediency. The playboy had a lunch date.

That moment was the first time she'd ever doubted his professionalism. Even then, the suspicion wasn't straightforward. Back in Australia, she'd had opportunities to insert VP shunts and she was competent in the procedure. He would have known that, so the fact he wasn't going to be in the operating theatre with her wasn't exactly abandoning his patient. Yet he'd admitted to going to lunch!

So, you'll lambast him for telling the truth when he could have created excuses like your previous bosses?

Sick of the endless loop of contradictory thoughts, Claire gave herself a shake. 'Today's a new day,' she said cryptically to Victoria's question, 'with new things to learn.'

'Alistair's a generous teacher.'

'He's certainly generous,' she said, fighting the urge to purse her lips in disapproval.

Victoria laughed and her chestnut ponytail swung around her shoulders. 'Our Alistair certainly loves women. That's what I wanted to talk to you about.'

Unable to hide her astonishment, Claire blinked at the pretty paramedic. *Not you too!* If the hospital grapevine was to be believed, Victoria and Dominic MacBride were very much together. 'Oh?' she asked cautiously.

Victoria's face lit up with enthusiasm. 'You've heard about the hospital ball?'

For anyone not to have heard about the ball, they'd have to have been living under a rock. Posters graced every noticeboard inside the hospital, and outside they'd been pasted on the poster pillars along the main road. Invitations had been sent to the past and present medical and auxiliary staff and one massive wall in the cafeteria had been covered with an enormous banner declaring the Spring Fling ball to be *the* social event of the season. The chatter about it had even managed to dent the football conversations about which team would be playing in the FA Cup final in a few weeks.

'I think I may have seen a poster about it somewhere,' she said with mock thoughtfulness.

Victoria missed the joke and continued in earnest. 'It's our first major event and we're hoping to raise fifty thousand pounds. The thing is, we really need Alistair to attend. If he doesn't, it's going to affect ticket sales.'

Claire laughed and then stopped as she caught the expression on Victoria's face. 'You're serious?'

'Deadly. He told Dominic that things were—' she raised her fingers into quotation marks '—complicated, which is code for he's broken some poor deluded girl's heart once again.' She let out a long sigh. 'Why they even think they could be the one to get him to commit is beyond me. The man is Peter Pan. Anyway, we really need him at the ball because we plan to auction the seat next to him. Women will have the chance to sit next to him for one of three courses. We're also selling his dance card. Your job is to make sure he attends.'

'I doubt I can make Alistair North do anything he doesn't want to do,' she replied honestly.

Victoria shot her an understanding smile. 'Alistair was raised right and he went to the right schools. As a result, he has a social code of conduct that he sticks to. He will go to the ball if he's your date.'

Claire's intake of breath was so sharp it sent her into a paroxysm of coughing. 'I can't ask my boss out,' she said, her voice rising sharply.

Victoria shrugged as if the fact Alistair was her boss was immaterial. 'Of course you can.

We all have to do our bit to save the castle,' she said pragmatically. 'Besides, it's all about how you word the invitation. Guilt him into it if you have to. Tell him it's imperative there's a show of strength from Koala Ward. He can't really argue against the expectation that as head of the department he should be there.'

The thought of having this conversation with Alistair North was enough to make her hyperventilate. 'Victoria, I really don't think—'

'Do you know how much the community will suffer if the hospital's sold?' Victoria's hands hit her hips, elbows akimbo. 'Keeping the castle open means everything to me, to the staff and to the patients. We're expecting to raise at least a thousand pounds by auctioning off his dance card, plus all the money we'll get for selling the seats next to him.'

Oh, how she wanted to rush to the ATM right this second and withdraw the cash but the idea of eating next month took precedence. 'I can't promise you—'

'Yes, you can. And you will,' Victoria said with the sort of authority in her voice usually reserved for recalcitrant patients. She reached out her hand and gave Claire's arm a gentle squeeze. 'And all the children and families in the district will thank you.'

Claire, who towered over the brunette, couldn't

comprehend how someone so petite could be such an indomitable force. 'That's blackmail,' she said weakly.

Victoria smiled. 'No. It's preventing a travesty. We're all mucking in to save our wonderful hospital for generations to come. This is your small contribution.'

Small? If this was small, she hated to think what a big request would look like. Claire was keen to do her bit, but she knew that Victoria had just well and truly dropped her into the muck right up to her neck.

CHAPTER THREE

CLAIRE STOOD AT the end of Ryan Walker's bed and chewed her lip. She had expected the little boy to have improved much faster than this. When he'd arrived at A & E barely conscious after being hit on the head by a falling beam at the Westbourne Primary School fire, Dominic MacBride, the castle's trauma surgeon, had immediately called her and Alistair in to consult. They'd ordered a CT scan that showed Ryan had sustained a fractured skull. Fortunately, there was no displacement of bones but thcre was a tiny associated subdural haematoma.

Rather than rushing in with guns blazing, she'd totally agreed with Alistair's conservative treatment plan. They'd worked closely with Rupert Emmerson, the anaesthetist, who'd sedated and ventilated Ryan. Alistair had inserted an intracranial pressure monitor and she'd inserted a central line, administering a mannitol infusion to decrease any associated brain swelling from the injury. The small haematoma hadn't diminished in size but neither had it grown. As a result, Ryan remained ventilated and his condition was still in a state of flux.

Yesterday morning, in a moment of frustrated despair during teaching rounds, she'd asked Alistair if she'd missed anything. Despite the large group of students gathered around the little tacker's bed, Alistair's pewter-grey eyes had zeroed in on her as if they were the only two people in the room.

'If you've missed something, Mitchell, then so have I.'

'Shall we do another MRI?'

'He had an MRI two days ago. While his observations remain the same it's not warranted. You have to ask yourself why you're doing the test.'

Because I have to do something. Doing nothing feels like giving up.

'Surely there's another option?'

Something she'd been momentarily tempted to think was sympathy had crossed his face but it vanished the moment he opened his mouth.

'There is. We wait.'

Wait? That wasn't something. That was sitting on their hands. 'And what if he doesn't improve?'

His shoulders had risen and fallen. 'That may be the reality.'

No. 'I don't like that reality,' she'd said briskly as if being terse would change it.

He'd given her a brief sad smile before returning his attention to the group of students. 'Who can tell me the elements of the Glasgow Coma Scale?'

'I swear he squeezed my hand before,' Ryan's mother said, her voice breaking into Claire's thoughts. Louise's anxious face was lined with two weeks of worry. 'That's a good sign, isn't it.'

It wasn't framed as a question—it was a solid statement. Louise needed to reassure herself that her little boy really was showing signs of improvement when in fact he was neither improving nor deteriorating. It was the limbo that was so disconcerting and heartbreaking, especially when neither she nor Alistair could pinpoint the reason.

Claire didn't want to upset the traumatised woman but she didn't attach the same significance to what was likely a muscle spasm. 'He's very heavily sedated, Louise.'

Claire checked his vital signs as she did twice each day. *No change.* She wrote up a drug order to override the one that was about to expire and then she turned her attention to Louise. Gunmetal-grey shadows stretched from the mother's eyes down to her cheekbones. Claire was familiar with the signs of relatives at the end of their rope.

'How are you sleeping?' she asked, despite the signs that the woman wasn't sleeping very much at all.

The exhausted mother shrugged and tilted her head towards the rollaway bed. 'It's got springs in interesting places.'

'We can get you another one,' Claire offered, having no idea if that was even possible. With all the talk of the probable sale of the hospital land and relocating the facility to one of the home counties, the powers that be weren't spending any money. If push came to shove, she'd buy a rollaway bed herself. At least it would feel like she was doing something other than this interminable waiting.

Louise sighed. 'To be fair, it's as much the disturbed sleep as anything. I wake up every time the nurses do their hourly check.'

'Would you consider taking a night off?' Claire asked carefully. She'd learned to tread very gently with families.

'I doubt I'd sleep any better at home.'

'Your GP can prescribe some sleeping tablets. Believe me, eight hours sleep in your own bed would do you the world of good.'

Louise gave her head a brisk shake. 'I want to be here when he wakes up.'

'I understand.' She pulled up a chair and sat, putting herself at eye level with Louise. 'The thing is, Ryan doesn't have to be alone. I'm sure there's someone in your extended family you could ask to give you a break? You know, so both you and Colin can get a full night's sleep.'

Louise glanced between Claire and her red-headed son, whose freckles seemed darker than ever against his porcelain-white face. A tear spilled over and ran down her cheek. 'I'm beyond making decisions. My mind feels like it's encased in a wet, London fog.'

'Then let me make the decision for you.'

She looked uncertain. 'I've never felt this exhausted in my life. It's like fatigue's not only invaded my soul but it's set up residence. All I want to do is curl up under the duvet and sleep for a week. I want to forget about the fire and how it turned my life on its head in an instant. But how can I? This is my new reality. Ryan can't leave and forget. If I go home, aren't I letting him down?'

Claire had heard variations of this story from grieving parents many times before. She gave the woman's knee a gentle pat. 'If you don't look after yourself, Louise, you risk getting sick. If you fall apart, then you'll be away from Ryan a lot longer than twelve hours.'

The enervated mother suddenly sagged as if

utterly defeated by a fortnight's emotional trauma and associated sleep debt. Her weary moss-green eyes met Claire's. 'If he wakes up while I'm at home, you must call me.'

'Of course.'

'Thank you.' The woman visibly brightened. 'Perhaps my leaving will trigger him waking up. You know, like when you take an umbrella with you every day and it's always dry but the moment you leave it at home it rains.'

Claire couldn't quite see the connection.

'I've been here for days,' Louise explained, 'and nothing's changed. It stands to reason that if I leave, he'll sit up and start talking.'

A worrying sensation roved along Claire's spine and she had to resist the urge not to wince. 'Medicine doesn't really work that way, Louise,' she said gently. 'Would you like me to contact your GP about the sleeping tablets? And I can ask the ward clerk to call you a taxi.'

'Thank you. That would be great.' Louise leaned over, brushed the hair from Ryan's forehead and kissed him. 'See you soon, buddy.' She smoothed his hair back into place and then stood up. 'Promise me, Claire, you'll telephone if he wakes up.'

'I promise,' Claire said easily. 'Wild horses couldn't stop me from giving you good news like that.'

* * *

Alistair high-fived Tristan Lewis-Smith. 'Way to go, Tris,' he said with a grin.

The kid had just whooped him at virtual tennis—twice—but he didn't care. He was too busy rejoicing in the fact that the ten-year-old had been seizure free for a week. That hadn't happened in two years and it was moments like these that reminded him that what he did each day mattered. Hell, it reinforced his mantra that every single day mattered and life should be lived to the full.

He'd almost lost the opportunity to do that, and when he'd woken up in the coronary care unit, he'd vowed never to forget how life could change in a heartbeat—or the lack of one as the case may be—and how close he'd come to death. He'd been blessed with a second chance and he never took it for granted. He was thrilled to be able to give Tristan a second chance at a normal life.

'Right-oh, mate.' He pulled down the sheet and patted the centre of the bed. 'Time to tuck in and pretend to read or the night sister will have my guts for garters.'

Full of beans and far from quiet, Tristan bounced onto the bed. 'You're just saying that because you're scared if you play another game I'll beat you. Again.'

'There is that,' Alistair said with a grin. 'Hurry up. I've got somewhere I need to be.'

Tristan scrambled under the covers. 'Nurse Saunders said you couldn't stay long because you've got a hot date.'

'Did she now?' Funny that Lindsay appeared to know more about this hot date than he did. He found himself automatically tucking the sheet around the little boy, only this time an odd feeling of something akin to emptiness accompanied it.

He immediately shook it off. He had no reason to feel empty or lonely. Life was good. He had a job he loved and a spacious and light-filled apartment just off the Portobello Road that he'd filled with curios from his world travels. Three years ago, he'd added to his property portfolio and bought a pretty stone cottage surrounded by fields of lavender in Provence. When he was there, he revelled in the sensory delights of sunshine, hearty Mediterranean food and great wine. He visited at least once a month, either alone or with a companion depending on whether or not the woman he was dating was still focused on having fun. The moment a woman started dropping hints about 'taking things to the next level' she was no longer welcome in France. Or in Notting Hill for that matter.

He loved women but he didn't do next levels. It was better to break a heart in the early days, well before things got serious, than to risk shattering a life, or worse, lives. His childhood was a case in point, and furthermore, no one ever knew precisely the duration of a second chance.

Surprised by the unexpected direction his musings had taken him—he didn't do dark thoughts and he certainly wasn't known for them—he left Tristan's room and contemplated the hour. It wasn't quite eight. As it was a Thursday night there'd be a sizeable hospital crowd at the Frog and Peach and he'd be welcomed with open arms for his dart skills. Oddly, the thought didn't entice. He had an overwhelming urge to do something completely different. Something wild that would make him feel alive.

Parkour in the dark?

Alive not dead, thank you very much.

Still, parkour in daylight this coming weekend was worth investigating. He pulled out his phone and had just brought up a browser when he heard, 'G'day, Alistair.'

Astonished, he spun around at the sound of the broad Australian accent. Although he'd heard Claire Mitchell use the informal Aussie greeting with other people, she'd always been far more circumspect with him. Well, with the exception of one or two lapses. In general, he knew she tried to be polite with him and that she found it a struggle. Did it make him a bad person that he enjoyed watching her keep herself in check? The woman was always buttoned up so tightly it wasn't surprising she cracked every now and then.

Now she stood in front of him with her hands pressed deep into the pockets of her once starched but now very end-of-day limp doctor's coat. Her hair was pulled back into its functional ponytail and a hot-pink stethoscope was slung around her neck. A tiny koala clung to her security lanyard along with a small pen on retractable elastic. Her utilitarian white blouse and medium length black skirt were unremarkable except that the skirt revealed those long shapely legs that taunted him.

Her feet were tucked into bright red shoes with a wide strap that crossed her instep just below her ankle and culminated in a large red button that drew the eye. He suddenly understood completely why Victorian gentlemen had waxed lyrical over a fleeting glimpse of a fine ankle.

He scanned her face, looking for clues as to why she was suddenly attempting a colloquial greeting with him. 'G'day, yourself,' he intoned back, with a fair crack at an Aussie accent.

Behind her sexy librarian-style glasses her eyes did that milk and dark chocolate swirly thing he always enjoyed and—was she blushing?

'Do you have a minute?' she asked, quickly pushing her glasses up her nose as they continued walking towards the lifts.

'Always. Problem?'

'Um.' She surreptitiously glanced along the corridor, taking in the nurses' station that was teaming with staff. She suddenly veered left into the treatment room.

Utterly intrigued by this uncharacteristic behaviour, he followed. 'Shall I close the door?'

She tugged hard at some stray strands of her hair before pushing them behind her ears. 'Thanks.'

He closed the door and flicked the blinds to the closed position before leaning back against the wide bench. Claire stood a metre or more away, her plump lips deliciously red. He shifted his gaze and— *Damn it!* His eyes caught on a fluttering pulse beating at the base of her throat. She really had the most gloriously long, smooth neck that just begged to be explored.

That's as may be, but remember, most of the time she's a pain in the ass. Not to mention she's your trainee.

'Alistair,' she started purposefully, and then stopped.

'Claire.' He couldn't help teasing back. He'd never seen her at a loss before and it was deliciously refreshing.

She took in such a deep breath that her breasts rose, stressing the button he was pretty certain sat just above her bra line. Was it delicate sheer lace or plainly utilitarian? It was his experience that plain women often wore the sexiest underwear.

With that mouth, she's hardly plain.

As if on cue, the tip of her tongue peeked out, flicking the bow of her top lip.

His blood leapt.

She cleared her throat. 'I hope you won't take this the wrong way but...'

Trying to look utterly unaffected by her, he cocked one brow and reminded himself of all the times she'd been critical of him. 'My sensibilities haven't stopped you from giving me your opinion before.'

This time she definitely blushed, but somehow she managed to wrestle her embarrassment under control with dignity. 'True, but that was work. This doesn't exactly fall into that category. Although I suppose it does technically if you—'

'You're babbling,' he said, hoping it would force her to focus. At the same time, he had an absurd and unexpected need to rescue her from herself.

Her head jerked up so fast he was worried her neck might snap but then she hit him with a gimlet stare. He forced himself not to squirm as an unsettling feeling trickled through him. Did she see straight through the man he liked to show the world? Had she glimpsed the corner edge of the bubbling mess he kept securely sealed away?

'As the head of the department of neurosurgery,' she said tightly, 'I think it's important you lead by example and attend the Spring Fling.'

The Spring Fling? Surely he'd misheard. 'You mean the neurosurgery spring symposium?'

She shook her head and once again the blush bloomed on her cheeks. She swallowed and that damn tongue of hers darted out to moisten her lips. This time as the zip of heat hit him, he pushed off the bench to try and shake it off.

'I mean the fundraising ball,' she said slowly, as if the words were being reluctantly pulled out of her.

He couldn't resist. 'Are you inviting me to the ball?'

Her eyes widened in consternation. 'No!' For a moment, indignation spun around her before fading with a sigh and a fall of her shoulders. 'I mean perhaps. Yes. In a manner of speaking.'

His mouth twitched. 'It's good to know you're so decisive.'

Her chin shot up, jabbing the air. 'You can tease me all you like, Mr—Alistair, but you know as well as I do that at the bare minimum there should be a neurosurgery staff table at the ball.'

Damn it to hell. She was absolutely right but how had she found out he wasn't going? He'd been keeping that bit of information to himself, more out of embarrassment than anything else.

A couple of months ago, just before Claire had arrived, he'd had a particularly tough day. He'd lost a patient—a two-year-old boy with a brain-stem glioma—and for some reason he'd avoided the sympathetic eyes of his staff at the Frog and Peach. He'd hit a trendy bar in Soho instead, and in retrospect, he'd consumed one whisky too many.

It had been enough to scramble his usually accurate *crazy woman* detector. As a result, he'd allowed himself to be tempted by the Amazonian features of Lela. The thirty-year-old was a fitness instructor as well as being a part-time security guard. They'd had a lot of fun together until he'd realised her possessive streak wasn't limited to bedroom games.

He knew the ball committee had flagged the idea of auctioning off the chairs next to eligible bachelors. Usually he'd have been fine with the concept and embraced it, but he'd been worried Lela might turn up and cause a nasty public spectacle. Or worse, buy the ticket. To save himself, and the hospital, embarrassment he'd decided not to attend the ball but to make a sizeable donation to the cause instead. The only person he'd mentioned this plan to was Dominic.

Stupid, stupid, stupid! The paediatric trauma surgeon had obviously broken the bro code and told Victoria. What was it about a man in love that made him prepared to throw his friend under the bus just to stay in sweet with his lady? Now the *i*-dotting and *t*-crossing Claire Mitchell was calling him out on a perceived lack of social etiquette.

He ploughed his hand through his hair. He'd been raised on etiquette, and the irony that an Australian, with their supposedly classless society, was reminding him of his social responsibilities almost made him laugh. Perhaps he could turn this whole Lela-and-the-ball mess around and use it to his advantage.

'Let me get this straight,' he said with a lazy smile. 'You're prepared to spend an evening with me just to make sure I do the right thing?'

This time she was the one to raise an eyebrow. 'As your second-in-command, I can't expect you to attend the ball if I'm not prepared to attend.'

'Ah, yes, that sucker duty gets you every time.'

She stiffened. 'But it seems you're often immune.'

Ouch. Her words tried to scratch him like the sharp tip of a knife, but he didn't need to justify himself to her. He was very well aware of his duty. Ironically, duty had arrived in a rush just after he'd vowed to make the most of every new day that had been gifted to him. It was the juxtaposition of his life.

'None of us are immune, Claire. It's just I try to have a bit of fun too.'

She narrowed her eyes. 'And you're inferring that I don't have fun?'

Not that I've seen. 'Have you had any fun since arriving in London?'

She looked momentarily nonplussed. 'I…um… yes. Of course.'

Liar. But he was planning on having some fun with her right now and killing two birds with one stone. 'Excellent. I can certainly promise you fun at the ball. Especially considering how you've gone above and beyond the call of duty and bought the seat next to me.'

'What?' She paled, her expression momentarily aghast, and then she rallied. 'I don't get paid enough for that.'

'Brutal.' He exaggeratedly slapped his chest in the general area of his heart, his long fingers grazing the lower edge of his pacemaker. 'And here I was thinking I was your date. I tell you what. I'll pay for both of our tickets.'

'That won't be necess—'

'It's the least I can do,' he interrupted, waving away her protest. 'I imagine it was Victoria who dropped you right in it.'

She grimaced. 'You're not wrong there.'

He made a huffing sound more at the absent

Dominic than her. 'The good thing is you'll be saving me from having to play nice all evening.'

Effrontery streaked across her face. 'Well, when you put it like that, I can hardly wait,' she said drily.

Her sarcasm was unexpected and delightfully refreshing and he heard himself laugh. He wasn't used to a woman viewing an evening with him as a trial. The women he dated erred on the appreciative side and often went to great lengths to make him happy. Not Claire Mitchell.

A streak of anticipation shot through him. Without realising it, she'd just thrown down a challenge. He wasn't totally convinced she was even capable of having fun and he had a sudden urge to know what she looked like when she was in the midst of a good time.

She'd smile like she did when you let her operate solo. Remember how you felt then?

He disregarded the warning that it was probably unwise to be looking forward to the ball quite this much.

'So will you be picking me—' His phone rang with the ICU ringtone, and as he pulled it from his pocket, Claire's pager beeped.

'North,' he said, answering the call just as Claire mouthed to him, 'ICU?'

Listening to the nurse on the other end of the line, he nodded at Claire and opened the treatment room door. As she walked quickly past him, her crisp scent of the sea drifted back to him and he was suddenly back on Bondi Beach when his life had been simpler and there had been few restraints placed upon it.

'We're on our way,' he told the worried nurse. Stepping out into the corridor, he followed Claire down the fire escape, taking the fastest way to ICU.

CHAPTER FOUR

CLAIRE WALKED OUT of the operating theatre, tugging her mask from her face. Her hand shook so much that her toss missed the bin and she had to stoop to pick up the mask. Even then it took her two more shots to land it.

Get a grip.

'You all right, Dr Mitchell?' Cyril, the night cleaner, asked. Apparently, he'd been working at the castle for forty years and as well as keeping the operating theatre suite clean he took a keen parental interest in the junior staff. 'You look a bit shaky.'

'Nothing a cup of tea won't fix,' she lied breezily, not trusting herself to let his concern touch her. She couldn't afford to fall apart. Not yet anyway. Not when her job was only half finished.

She walked into the doctors' lounge, which at ten in the evening was thankfully empty. She needed and wanted privacy to make this call. Picking up the phone, it took her two attempts to get the number right as her mind kept spinning off and practicing what she was going to say. As the phone rang in her ear, she concentrated on slowing her breathing and her wildly hammering heart.

'Hello,' a sleep-filled voice croaked down the line.

'Louise.' Her voice sounded unsteady and she tried to firm it up. 'It's Claire Mitchell. From the hospital.'

'Claire!' Ryan's mother's voice was instantly alert. 'You're calling me? Oh, my God,' she said half laughing, half crying, 'it's just like the umbrella story. You told me to come home and now you're calling. He's awake, isn't he? Colin, wake up. It's Ryan.'

Claire's stomach lurched so hard she had to force the rising tide of acid back down her throat. 'Louise,' she said firmly but gravely, trying to signal to the woman this call wasn't the positive one she craved. 'Ryan's not awake.'

'What?' She sounded confused. 'Then why are you calling?' she asked angrily.

Claire thought about the desperately ill little boy who was lying surrounded by all the latest medical technology. 'Ryan's condition has deteriorated.'

'No!'

Claire flinched at the pain contained in one small word.

'You said you'd call me if he woke up.' Louise's accusation was loud and clear. In the mother's mind, Claire had broken a promise to her.

'I'm sorry to have to tell you that Ryan's had another bleed. We rushed him to theatre and we've just operated on him.'

'So, this is a just a little setback? He's going to be all right?'

Claire bit her lip so hard she tasted blood. 'Unfortunately, it was a big bleed. It caused his brain to swell and it was necessary to remove a small part of his skull to ease the pressure. It's called a craniotomy.'

'He's got a hole in his head?'

The rising disbelief and trauma in Louise's voice wound through her like poison. 'The bone flap's being stored in a freezer at the hospital until the swelling in Ryan's brain has subsided. When that happens, we can reinsert it.'

'Are you saying that his brain's open to the air? That can't possibly be a good thing.'

'He'll wear a special protective helmet while the bone flap's removed.'

There was a long silence followed by a sharp intake of breath. 'He's not going to have brain damage, is he?'

This was the question Claire always dreaded.

'We won't know the exact situation until the swelling in his brain has diminished.'

'How long will that take?'

'I'm sorry, Louise, but right now I can't say. It's too hard to predict.'

She heard the sound of a duvet being moved and feet hitting the floor. 'Why didn't you see this coming? Why didn't you stop it?'

The words whipped and lashed Claire, playing on her days of misgivings that they were missing something. 'I know this is very hard for you—'

'Hard!' Louise barked down the phone, her voice so loud and outraged that Claire jumped. 'Do you have children, Claire?'

Don't play this game. You'll be the one left bleeding. Even if Louise had been a friend instead of a patient's relative, Claire wouldn't have confessed her one regret. Somehow, by pursuing the toughest medical speciality to prove to herself, Gundiwindi and the world that she was capable and intelligent, she was suddenly thirty-four, alone and with the chance of motherhood rapidly diminishing.

Alistair walked into the lounge and threw her a questioning glance as he cast tea bags into mugs.

Claire turned away from his penetrating gaze, which despite her determined efforts to stay on task had the uncanny ability to derail her concentration every single time. It both bothered and confused her. She'd always been known for her intense focus and her ability to block out all unnecessary distractions. Over the last few years, her consultants had told her that her natural attention to detail was a perfect trait for a neurosurgeon.

No one outside of her family knew that skill wasn't natural at all but borne from necessity and honed by sheer determination and bloody-mindedness. It rarely let her down. Even during what she'd considered the 'heady days' with Michael, when she'd thought he loved her, her focus hadn't faltered. However, under the assault of Alistair North's clear, iron-ore-grey eyes, it wobbled precariously.

'Louise,' she said, centring her thoughts. 'Ryan's being transferred back to ICU now. When you and your husband arrive at the hospital, Mr North and I will be here to answer all your questions. Just ask the staff to page us.'

She finished the call and slowly lowered the receiver onto the cradle. She knew she should stand up but she wasn't certain her shaking legs would hold her.

'Tough call,' Alistair commented as he opened the fridge.

'I've had better.'

'Do you take milk and sugar in your tea?'

Despite her surprise at his offer, her head fell

back to rest on the couch as exhaustion caught up with her. 'Just milk.'

'You look like you could do with some sugar.'

She suddenly craved something sweet. 'Do you have chocolate?'

'Surely in the six weeks you've been here you've learned that any chocolate that enters this room vanishes in five minutes.' He rummaged through the cupboards and then gave an unexpected woot, holding up a red-and-black box. 'Will chilli and chocolate shortbread suffice?'

She had a ridiculous and overwhelming urge to cry at his unanticipated thoughtfulness. 'Awesome.'

He walked over to her carrying two mugs of tea and balancing the box of biscuits on the top of one of the mugs. 'Here you go.'

There was no sign of the teasing playboy or the supercilious consultant. In her overwrought state, she couldn't make sense of the change and that troubled her. She stuck to what she knew best: work. 'We should have done that MRI.'

Her words tumbled out loaded with blame. 'We should have done more. We caused this.'

'Hey,' he said, his grey eyes suddenly stern. 'We did not cause this. We both operated on him and we both saw exactly the same thing. This bleed was hidden by the original haematoma. That's why it wasn't showing up on the scans.

On the plus side, if he'd bled anywhere else instead of in ICU, he'd probably be dead.'

Culpability pummelled her so hard it hurt and she was unable to control her belligerent tone. 'How is that supposed to make me feel better? He wouldn't have been in hospital if it weren't for the fire. We're supposed to pre-empt disasters like this. Now he's sicker than when he arrived.'

'Not necessarily,' Alistair said with frustrating logic and calm. 'The craniotomy gives him the possibility of recovery. We've done everything we can to give him a chance at the best possible outcome.' His face softened into friendly lines. 'I know this sucks, but it's just one of those god-awful things that happen sometimes.'

'I don't accept that,' she said so emphatically her hand jerked. Hot tea spilled over the rim and onto her skin. 'Ouch!'

He immediately removed the mug from her hand. 'I'll get you some ice. Meanwhile, open wide.' He shoved a shortbread into her mouth.

For reasons she couldn't fathom, she'd done as he'd asked and obediently opened her mouth. Now, more out of surprise than anything else, she bit into the soft, buttery, chocolate goodness and embraced the kick of chilli. It shocked her senses in a much-needed way and she wiped her tea-covered hand on her scrub. A large red welt with a white centre rose fast on the base of her thumb accompanied by a furious sting. Wearing surgical gloves was going to hurt for the next few days.

Alistair returned with an icepack wrapped in a red-and-white-checked tea towel. His large hand folded the pack around hers and the burn of the ice tangoed with the burn of his hand. He lifted her left hand and placed it over the pack. 'Hold that there for ten minutes.'

'Thanks.' Irrational tears threatened again along with an equally irrational sense of loss as he removed his hand. *What the hell was wrong with her?*

'Shortbread sugar starting to hit?' Alistair asked, his brow furrowed with mild concern.

Not really. Her head was spinning and she felt strangely adrift and utterly drained. It was as if a decade of fatigue had just sideswiped her. She'd been working so hard and for so long doing everything on her own, proving she was as good as or better than her peers, and fighting harder than anyone to stay on top that she wasn't used to anyone looking out for her. Right now, nothing was making sense, especially this version of Alistair who was being remarkably kind.

Her entire body sagged heavily and it took almost more effort than she had to keep herself upright. She had a ludicrous urge to drop her head onto his shoulder and take shelter there, sleeping for a week.

Have you completely lost your mind? You're at work. He's your boss and just no. *Got that?*

Aghast that her jumbled thoughts had somehow managed to get to this point, she tried squaring her shoulders in an attempt to summon up her professional decorum. Not once in her career had she ever lost control at work and tonight wasn't the time to start—especially not in front of Alistair North. No, the moment the ten minutes was up, she'd stow the ice pack in the freezer, bid Alistair a crisp goodnight and head home to bed for a much-needed sleep. Everything would make sense again after a good night's sleep.

And if it doesn't?

She'd worry about that if and when it happened.

Alistair rubbed the back of his neck, slightly bewildered and definitely disconcerted by this version of Claire Mitchell sitting next to him on the couch. Her reaction to what had been a routine craniotomy was out of proportion and out of character. When he'd first met her, he'd picked her as being meticulous, ambitious and with a 'take no prisoners' approach to work. It wasn't that she didn't care—she was indeed empathetic—but she always put the medicine first. Surely Ryan Walker's unexpected deterioration couldn't have been the first time she'd been faced with an un-answerable medical conundrum?

Whatever it was, it was obvious it had upset her greatly. As her consultant, it was his job to help her work through it. But how? He sipped his tea and pondered the matter until a possible solution came to him.

'Would it help if we took Ryan's case to peer review? I doubt they'll disagree with our treatment plan but the process will reassure you that we did everything we could.'

'Peer review doesn't have to deal with Ryan's parents,' she said, her voice cracking. Her shoulders slumped. 'Louise Walker hates me.'

Ah. So Claire Mitchell wasn't just about protocol and paperwork after all. Underneath her automaton tendencies and prickly exterior existed a regular person. For whatever reason, something about Ryan's case had got under her skin. He knew all about that. At some point in every doctor's career, one patient would touch them more than the others. 'Louise Walker is a terrified mother.'

'I know.'

Her eyes, now as round as huge saucers of warm caramel, looked at him. He got an unanticipated urge to dive right in. *That won't help matters. You don't really like her.* Baffled, he blinked and then as his vision came back into focus he saw her beseeching distress urging him to understand.

'I made Louise leave the hospital today. I insisted on it.'

He rushed to reassure her and at the same time get himself back on solid ground. 'And rightly so. The woman was exhausted.'

Her fingers plucked at invisible balls of lint on her scrubs. 'She made me promise to call her if Ryan woke up.'

Worry pulled tightly behind his eyes. 'Promises are always fraught…'

Her chin, which he'd noticed tended to tilt up sharply whenever she felt under attack, barely lifted. 'I'm not a novice.'

'No.'

'And of course I'd have called her if Ryan woke up. It was hardly an unprofessional assurance.'

Suddenly, his veil of confusion lifted. With piercing clarity, he saw exactly where this was going. He felt for her—he really did. 'When you rang Louise just before, she thought—'

'That I had the first piece of good news in two weeks.' She sucked her lips in tight and blinked rapidly. It wasn't enough to prevent a tear escaping and running down her cheek beyond the reach of her glasses. She crooked the forefinger of her uninjured hand and brushed it away.

Bloody hell. Unlike a lot of men who froze in

the presence of a distressed woman, he was always moved to assist, which was why he'd already made his registrar a cup of tea. But now, seeing the usually stitched-up and almost too-together Claire Mitchell falling apart in front of him sent a visceral spike of pain into him, cramping his gut. 'Why didn't you ask me to make the call?'

Her free hand curled into a tight fist and her chin dropped towards her chest. 'You were very clear about it being my job.'

'Bloody hell, Claire,' he said softly, the words coming out on a puff of air. He felt like the worst boss in the world. 'I don't understand. You've queried me and judged my opinions more than once in the past few weeks. Why on earth did you decide this telephone call was the *one* thing you weren't going to question?'

'All I know,' she said so softly he needed to strain to listen, 'is that I've destroyed Louise Walker. I've made her pain ten times worse.'

Her head rose and her woebegone expression ate into him like acid on paper. It was as natural as breathing to put a hand on her shoulder. 'You haven't destroyed her,' he said quietly.

Her head fell forward onto his shoulder and he patted her gently on the back. 'Deep down you know that. You're just having a rough night.'

She made a muffled noise that sounded half

like denial and half like a hiccough. He smiled at the very normal snorting sound coming from someone he'd thought kept a wide distance between work and her emotions. He found himself stroking her hair, the fine strands like silk against his palm. With her head now resting under his chin, the scent of cinnamon and apples drifted upwards.

Memories flooded back—a large homey kitchen warmed by the continually heating Aga, the beatific, round face of Cook and the aroma of brown sugar and butter. Everything he associated with the comfort of childhood was centred on that kitchen. Not once in his wildest dreams had he ever imagined it wouldn't always be there waiting for him when he returned home from boarding school. Twenty-six years had passed and he still missed it.

Claire raised her head, her cheeks blotchy and her eyes red-rimmed. Her gaze was fixed doggedly on the wet patch on his shirt and her small hand patted it as if the action was enough to dry it. 'Oh, God. I'm so sorry.'

The pads of her fingers warmed his skin through the fine cotton. 'No need to apologise,' he said, intending to sound hearty and encouraging, but the words came out husky as if he was suffering from a cold. 'Worse things have happened to my shirts.'

'The thing is, I've never done anything like this at work before.' She sounded utterly poleaxed. 'You must think I'm a total basket case.'

'No.' He knew he should say more. He should tell her that everyone has a bad day occasionally, that doctors are human too, and some cases have a deeper impact than others. But her heat was weaving through him and creating so much havoc that he was having trouble remembering his own name, let alone articulating anything beyond a single syllable. In a desperate attempt to regain his equilibrium, he caught her hand, encasing it in his, stopping her jerky strokes.

She stilled for a moment and stared at his white hand covering her tanned one and then, slowly, she lifted her face to his. Her liquid eyes were a mirror to her embarrassment, confusion and sorrow. Once again, he wanted to make her feel better, because anyone who worked in medicine had spent time in that dismal place and it was dangerous to linger there too long. He was about to say, 'Tomorrow's another day,' when he glimpsed something indefinable beyond the chaotic swirl of emotions. The shadows told him it wasn't new. In fact, it had the intransigent look of an indelible stain that no amount of soap, salt or methylated spirits could remove.

Was it doubt? Fear? Inadequacy? *Surely not*. But whatever it was, it hit him hard in the solar plexus and held on tight like a lasso. *Whatever it is, it's wrong. It shouldn't be part of her. It doesn't belong there.*

The need to vanquish this malignant thing and banish it from her eyes—from her soul—pulled him down towards her. His lips touched her damp cheek in a consoling kiss and the tang of salt zipped into him. He was about to pull back when her head turned and suddenly his mouth was softly touching those plump, ruby-red lips. They were soft and tear-cooled. He tasted the heady essence of bergamot.

Stop now.

He was about to pull back when her lips opened infinitesimally. He was immediately rushed by the unexpected spicy zap of chilli. Hot. Sizzling. One hundred per cent aroused woman. His breath left his lungs and for a moment he was rendered utterly still, unable to think, move or feel.

The tip of her tongue flicked against his lips so lightly and so quickly that his brain couldn't decide if it had even happened or if he was imagining it. But his body knew. Good God, it knew. He dropped his arms to her waist and hauled her in against him before opening his mouth and welcoming her in.

She came to him without a moment's hesitation, filling him completely. Her tongue explored, her teeth nipped, her heat and flavours exploded through him until he was nothing but a river of pulsating sensation. Her free hand wound its way through his hair, her fingers digging into his scalp as if she needed to hold on to something to keep herself tethered to earth.

He understood exactly. Kissing her was like being in free fall. He returned her kiss with one of his own—deep, thorough and practiced until he heard a low guttural moan coming from Claire. Usually that sound made him smile and reinforced not only that he knew exactly what he was doing but that he was the one in total control.

Not this time.

His usual measured composure with women was unravelling faster than a skein of wool in the paws of a cat. He had the strangest awareness that somehow she'd turned the tables on him completely. What had started out as a quick and reassuring kiss to console her was now a kiss that was stripping him of the protective layers he'd spent five years cementing into place.

Break the kiss. Now. Right now.

But his body overruled him again, craving what was on offer and seizing it like a drowning man grips a life preserver. He slid the utilitarian black band from her ponytail, and as her hair fell to her shoulders in a sun-kissed cascade, it released its treasured aroma of spices and apples. Golden strands caressed his face and he breathed deeply. Claire's sweet behind was now in his lap—he had no idea if he'd pulled her there, if she'd climbed in or if it was a bit of both. It didn't matter. All that mattered was here, now and her.

Her hand cupped the back of his neck, her fingers splayed. His hand, which had been gripping her hip, now slid under the loose top of her scrubs. His palm instantly tingled as it touched warm, smooth skin. He spider-walked his fingers along her spine, absorbing every rise and dip until he reached the wide strap of her bra.

He'd never considered any piece of lingerie a challenge—more like an inconvenient barrier that he dismantled easily every time. His fingers rested on the hooks and he was just about to flick and twist when Claire ripped her hand out of his and hauled her mouth from his lips. It all happened so fast that he shivered from the loss of her intoxicating heat.

Her lips, now bee-sting pouty and puffy from kissing and being kissed, gave her a sexy aura he'd never suspected even existed underneath her uptight personality. But despite how deliciously alluring it made her, it was the way her mussed hair fell softly, framing her face that got to him. It made her look younger than her years. She suddenly seemed fragile and vulnerable as if she expected the world as she knew it to end any second.

In that instant, he knew the exact direction her thoughts had taken. He was her boss and she was his trainee. Hospitals had rules about this sort of thing to protect both parties from sexual harassment charges. Without meaning to, they'd both fallen over the line together, but there was no power play happening on either side. He'd stake his life she was as surprised as he was that the kiss had even happened.

'It's okay, Claire,' he said, wanting to put her at ease, but his voice was rough, raspy and the antithesis of soothing.

'Okay?' Her voice rose with incredulity and her beautiful eyes reflected her turmoil. In a flurry of uncoordinated movements, which included her knee pressing into his inner thigh, she scrambled out of his lap as fast as if he was on fire and she was about to go up in flames too. The entire time she kept her arms outstretched in front of her as if she was scared he was going to try and touch her.

'I… This… It.' Her left hand covered her mouth for a moment before falling away. 'Nothing about any of this is okay.'

Still dazed from her kisses and with the majority of his circulating volume residing in his lap, he struggled to move beyond the basic functions of his reptilian brain. He tried a second time to reassure her. 'I meant, we're both adults.' He shrugged. 'Things happen.'

She shook her head so hard and fast that her hair whipped around her head in a golden wave. '*Nothing* happened.' Her voice trembled along with the rest of her. 'Do you understand? Absolutely nothing.'

As his blood pounded thickly through his body defying her words, both their pages beeped. The sound stopped Claire's flight to the door. 'Oh, no. The Walkers are here.'

'Right.' His voice sounded a long way away as his body lurched from lust to logic and the doctor overrode the man. Hell, he needed some time. 'I'll meet you in ICU in five minutes.'

Relief and embarrassment tugged at her cheeks. 'Yes. Good. Fine. I'll be there.' She disappeared into the corridor.

Well, that went well, Alistair. Blowing out a long, slow breath he rubbed his face with his hands and tried to fathom how something so incredible had ended so badly.

CHAPTER FIVE

'DECAF THIS MORNING, please, Tony.'

The friendly barista shot her a disbelieving look. 'Is not coffee, *mia bella*.'

She gave him an apologetic shrug. 'Please.' The last thing she needed was caffeine. It was barely seven and she was running on adrenaline. Her heart pounded, her chest was so tight breathing felt like lifting weights, she was as jumpy as a cat and she felt the telltale burn of reflux. That was always the stress marker.

Occasionally, when she thought work was going well, she'd be surprised to get the liver-tip pain telling her that her body wasn't as calm as her mind. Today, she didn't need her medical degree to know the exact cause of her extreme agitation. She'd relived the reason over and over and over last night until exhaustion had somehow managed to claim her, providing a few hours of fitful sleep.

She'd woken with a start to a foggy dawn and

the weight of reality crushing down on her so hard and heavy she was surprised she wasn't lying on the floor. Real life had decisively ended a wonderful dream where she'd felt unusually safe and secure. A utopia where she'd been able to be herself without the constant and nagging worry that someone was going to find out that despite all her hard work she was always only one step away from failing. Those tantalisingly peaceful feelings had vanished a second after she'd woken. Tranquillity had been torpedoed by the visual of her nestled in Alistair North's lap, kissing him like he was the last man standing after the apocalypse.

She'd jumped her boss. *Oh, God, oh, God, oh, God.*

Hours later, she still wasn't totally certain how it had happened.

Oh, come on. Be honest. Bottom line, you abandoned your principles, you opened your mouth and took what you wanted. You sucked Alistair North's marrow into you like he was oxygen.

She barely recognised the woman she'd been last night, and she knew if it had been an option, she'd have climbed inside the man. Never before had she let go like that, giving up all thought and reason, and existing only for the streaming sensations of bliss that had consumed her. It was if she'd been drawing her life force from him. She'd certainly never kissed anyone with such intensity before.

You've never been kissed like that before.

Her mind retreated from the thought so fast she almost gave herself whiplash. Truth be told, despite her thirty-four years, her kissing experience was fairly limited. During her teenage years, her brother's footy mates had considered her far too bookish and reserved to bother trying to kiss and her peers thought she was weird for studying so hard, so when she'd left Gundiwindi bound for Adelaide Uni, she'd been a kissing virgin as well as a sexual one.

It had only taken one medical students' society party to remedy the kissing situation. She'd discovered that having a tongue shoved unceremoniously down her throat by a drunk second year had been enough. Then and there shc'd determined to wait until she met someone who, A, she actually liked and, B, had some experience and panache in the art of kissing.

Michael had literally walked into her life five years later when she'd been hiking the Milford Track in the spectacular South Island of New Zealand. After two days spent laughing and talking together, and with him proffering the occasional hand to balance her as she crossed creeks and clambered over fallen trees, he'd kissed her on the sandy shore of Milford Sound with the backdrop of the indomitable Mitre Peak.

It had been the most romantic thing she'd ever experienced. For a while, all of Michael's romantic gestures had deluded her into thinking she was worthy of love after all. When the cracks started appearing, the more she worked to shore them up, the worse things had got. His parting words still haunted her. *You're too hard to love, Claire.*

Her alarm had chosen that moment to shrill, pulling her thoughts sharply and blessedly away from the past and dragging them firmly into the present. She'd run to the shower and left the flat half an hour later, walking directly to Tony's in the ubiquitous London mist.

The barista handed her the usual half dozen coffees pressed snugly into their cardboard carrier along with one extra. 'What's this?' she asked as her left hand wrapped around the single cup.

'A proper latte, *doctore*.'

'But, Tony, I wanted decaf.'

He tapped the cup with a *D* scrawled on it. 'Is here. But you drink it and I know you wish you get your usual.'

'Thanks.' He wasn't to know that if she were any more wired she'd shatter. She handed over some pound notes but he waved them away. 'The doctors at the castle, they fix my Serena when she born with her bad foot. Sick *bambinos* need the hospital. I happy to help.'

'That's very generous of you. I know the protestors on the night shift appreciate your coffee.'

She heard the gentle clearing of a throat behind her—the British equivalent of *Hurry up*.

'Bye, Tony.'

'*Ciao, bella*. You have a good day, yes.'

A good day. Oh, yeah. It was going to be one for the ages. More than anything she wanted a time machine so she could return to last night and change everything that had happened, starting with preventing little Ryan Walker from having a large brain bleed. At least the gods were on her side today in as much as it wasn't an operating day. The thought of having to stand next to Alistair—*Mr North, Mr North, Mr North.*

You're kidding yourself if you think using his title is going to give you any protection.

It's all I've got.

That and hiding from him as much as possible. Only she knew hiding was a pipe dream. The whole point of her scholarship was to work hand in glove with the man and learn as much from him as she possibly could. Last night, she'd left the hospital the moment the difficult interview with the Walkers was concluded. In fact, she'd been the first one to leave, with a brisk goodnight to her consultant in front of the distraught parents, blocking any chance of him saying anything to her about the kiss.

The only reprieve she had today was that straight after rounds he was working from home, preparing his paper for the neurosurgery symposium.

Yesterday morning when she'd read that entry in the electronic diary, she'd rolled her eyes. In not unexpected fashion, he'd left it pretty much to the last minute to get it done. If she'd been presenting a paper, she'd have had it fully edited, bound and memorised a week ahead of time because medicine had a habit of throwing curve balls. All it took was a couple of emergencies or some staff illness to throw out a timeline. She always padded her deadlines with a lot of wriggle room, as much to allow for her own set of learning challenges as well as for external ones.

Today, however, there was no eye rolling at Alis— Mr North's laid-back procrastination, only unbridled relief. It meant the only time she had to see him today was at the ICU and Koala Ward rounds. Given they'd be surrounded by staff and students and their focus would be on patient care, how hard could that be? He was hardly going to say anything to her about last night in front of everyone and she sure as hell wasn't going to mention it. Not now. Not ever. In regards to last night, her plan was to pretend and subsequently believe that it had *never* happened. She could only hope that Mr North felt the same.

Lost so deeply in her thoughts, she was surprised to find she'd arrived at the hospital. As she distributed the coffees, she made sure to mention to everyone they were a donation from Tony's Trattoria. Chatting with the protesters and learning more and more stories about the legacy of the castle was fast becoming a favourite part of her day and she listened with delighted fascination. A woman was telling a tale about her grandfather who'd been a surgeon during the Second World War. Claire was so busy listening to how he'd risked his own life to save others by operating in the basement of the hospital during the Blitz that she lost all sense of time.

Hearing someone's watch chime the hour, she gasped. *Late!* She hurriedly excused herself, ran through the gates, pelted up the D wing stairs, flung herself through the door and arrived on Koala Ward a panting and gasping mess.

Andrew Bailey gave her a wide-eyed look. 'You okay?'

She was desperately short of breath but she dug deep and summoned up a husky 'Fine' as she tried to fill her lungs with air. At the same time, she worked on quelling the rising tide of frantic dread that threatened to swamp her like a massive wave at Coogee. Being a few minutes late for rounds with a consultant who considered ten minutes after the hour as being 'on time' wasn't an issue. Being twenty minutes later than her usual arrival time was a disaster. It meant she had no time to read and memorise the overnight reports. It meant she'd be flying blind during rounds.

Panicked, she rounded on her house officer. 'Have you read the reports?'

'Was I supposed to?' Andrew asked, half bemused and half confused. 'I thought that was the point of rounds.'

Still trying to catch her breath, she huffed loudly and caught the injured look in her generally congenial junior's eyes. He was absolutely correct—for most people that was the case. 'True, but it never hurts to be ahead of the game and impress the consultant.'

A grin broke across his round face. 'Is that why you're here early most days?'

She dodged the truth with the skill of a secret keeper. 'Something like that.'

The rumble of many feet against the linoleum floor made her turn. Alistair North was striding along the corridor with the nurse unit manager and the nursing and medical students hurrying along behind.

Claire pressed her glasses up her nose and blinked. Alistair North didn't ever wear a white coat but he generally wore one of what she'd come to realise was a selection of fine wool Italian suits. Generally, he started the day in a jacket and tie, although the ties were never serious. They were almost always prints of animated characters from kids' TV shows, which the little patients loved. Claire's favourite ties were from a fundraising range sold by the castle's auxiliary. Some clever clogs had come up with the idea of printing the children's drawings of doctors, nurses and auxiliary staff onto silk. She particularly liked the one of a doctor wearing a head torch and a big smile.

Just admit it. You like that one because it's Alistair.

Not if my life depended on it.

By late afternoon most days, he was seen on the ward in scrubs, or if it was a non-operating day, he'd have discarded the jacket and tie. An open-necked business shirt was as casual as she'd ever seen him, but today there was no sign of a suit, nor smart casual weekend wear or even jeans. He was striding towards them wearing a T-shirt that stretched across his wide chest and perfectly outlined the rise and fall of his pectoral muscles. The shirt read *Epilepsy Warrior Run*. Her gaze instinctively dropped.

Damn. No compression tights.

Shut up! She hated the zip of disappointment

that wove through her that the rest of his body wasn't delineated in fine detail by tight fabric. His running shorts, however, only came to mid-thigh, giving her plenty of opportunity to admire his taut quads.

Look up, look up, look up.

'Morning, Mitchell. Bailey,' he said with his usual nod of greeting. 'Missed the two of you at boot camp this morning.'

'Boot camp, sir?' Andrew said faintly. The rotund house officer wore the look of one who went to great lengths to avoid any sort of physical pursuit.

'Yes, Bailey. All Koala Ward staff are participating in the Epilepsy Warrior fun run. Morag—' he turned to the highly efficient unit nurse manager '—you sent the diary entry to everyone about this morning's training session?'

'Of course,' she said briskly in her thick Scottish brogue.

Claire pulled out her phone and immediately saw the reminder on her screen. Her stomach fell through the floor. She'd been so obsessed by the fact she'd landed in Alistair's lap last night and tickled his tonsils that she'd totally forgotten about boot camp.

Andrew's face drained of colour. 'Surely someone needs to be on duty on—' he read the black and purple writing on his boss's T-shirt '—the tenth. Happy to volunteer, sir.'

'Already got that covered, Bailey,' Alistair said in a tone that brooked no argument. He swung his clear sea-grey gaze to Claire.

Be professional. She clenched her fists and willed herself not to drop her gaze. Willed herself to act as if this was just a regular morning instead of the one after her worst ever career folly. Memories of last night—of the way his eyes and then his mouth had fixed on hers—rolled back in, foaming and bubbling like a king tide.

Let it go. It didn't happen.

Oh, but it did. She had the sweet and tender bruises on her lips to prove it.

Now, faced with all six foot of him standing there in front of her wearing athletic gear and with the scent of his cologne invading her senses, it was increasingly difficult to focus on her plan to banish every delicious thing that had happened between them. *Remember the embarrassment. Remember he's your boss. That will do the trick every time.*

'It's not like you to forget an appointment, Mitchell,' he said, using her surname in the British public school way as he did occasionally. 'It's important we all attend for team spirit,' he added politely.

Despite the well-modulated parameters of his

very British accent, she heard the unmistakable tone of an order. Was this his way of saying that he agreed with her that last night was an aberration? That it was a shocking mistake they both needed to forget and move on from? That it was over and done with and she needed to remember that the cohesion of the workplace team always came ahead of everything?

Please let it be so. 'We won't let you down again,' she said brightly. She sent up a plea that Alistair had caught her double meaning and knew that she understood they were both on the same page about last night. 'We're looking forward to the next boot camp, aren't we, Andrew?'

Andrew stared at her as if she'd completely lost her mind. 'Wouldn't miss it,' he said glumly.

Alistair grinned and clapped his hands together once. 'Excellent. Let's start rounds.'

As they walked towards the first bay, Morag handed Claire a tablet computer. Archie McGregor's medical history was open on the screen, but before she could silently read the first sentence, Alistair was saying, 'Lead off, Dr Mitchell.'

Eight sets of eyes swung her way. Even before her mouth had dried, her tongue had thickened and her throat had threatened to close, the words on the screen had jumbled into an incomprehensible mess. Long ago voices boomed in her head, deafening her.

Moron. That girl's a sandwich short of a picnic.
Panic eddied out from her gut and into her veins, stealing her concentration. She broke out in a cold sweat. Her greatest fear, which lurked constantly inside her and was never far from the surface, surged up to choke her. *You knew you'd get found out one day. This is it.*

No! She'd fought too hard for it to end like this. She'd set up strategies so this situation would never happen to her and she wasn't about to let years of sacrifice go to waste and have it fall apart now. Not here in London where it was too easy for people to make cheap shots at her being a colonial. Not when she was the recipient of one of the most prestigious scholarships on offer for neurosurgery. Not when she was so close to qualifying.

Think!

'Actually,' she said, shoving the tablet at her junior houseman with a hand that trembled. 'Archie is Dr Bailey's patient. He admitted him overnight.'

Andrew, who'd accepted the tablet without question, glanced at the screen. 'Archie McGregor, age seven, admitted last night post-seizure and with suspected juvenile myoclonic epilepsy. Observations stable overnight and...'

Claire wanted to relax and blow out the breath that was stalled tightly in her chest but she didn't have any time to spare. As Andrew was fielding a battery of questions from Alistair, she was trying to calmly and surreptitiously read the next patient's history.

An hour later she was helping herself to a delicious currant bun from the nurses' breakfast platter. As she bit into the sticky sweetness, she gave thanks that she'd not only narrowly avoided disaster, she'd also survived the round. Alistair had appeared happy with both her and Andrew's treatment plans and now, emergencies excepted, her boss was gone for the day. She was thankfully home free. She had some medication charts to write up, some test results to read and then, fingers crossed, she was going to take advantage of the relative calm and spend some time in the library studying.

'Oh, good.' A very familiar voice rumbled around her, its timbre as rich and smooth as a Barossa Valley cabernet sauvignon. 'There you are.'

Shock stuck the sticky bun to the roof of her mouth and she tried desperately to dislodge it with a slurp of tea. The hot liquid went down the wrong way and she coughed violently, trying to get her breath. The next minute, Alistair's face was pushed in close to hers with his brows pulled down sharply.

'Can you get air?'

She shook her head but he misunderstood and the next minute the side of his hand sliced down between her shoulder blades like a karate chop. The snaps on her bra bit into her skin. 'Ouch.'

'Good,' he said, cheerfully reappearing back in front of her. 'I need you alive today.'

'Just today?' she said waspishly as the tangy scent of his sweat hit her nostrils. She worked hard at resisting the urge to breathe in deeply. 'I rather like being alive every day.'

'As do I. Live every day as if it's your last.'

She took a careful sip of tea. 'I've often found people who say that use it as an excuse to be self-ish.'

His smile faded and a line of tension ran along his jaw, disappearing up behind his ear. 'That's a very jaundiced view of humanity.'

She welcomed the familiar antagonism vibrating between them and relaxed into it, giving thanks that everything was back to normal. 'Not at all. It's merely an observation about how some people live their lives with little thought or regard for how their actions impact on others.'

His eyes darkened and he looked as if he was about to say something when he suddenly helped himself to a currant bun. She was oddly disappointed that he wasn't going to take the discussion further. Sparring in a robust debate with Alistair North was far safer than confiding in him.

Or kissing him.

She suddenly felt stranded standing there in the small pantry. She was far too aware of him and how his mouth, which had savoured hers so thoroughly last night, was now relishing the currant bun. Too aware of how his tight behind was pressed hard against the bench and how his long, running-fit legs stretched out in front of him. She suddenly wanted to invoke the staff dress code she'd been lectured on during her orientation program.

He raised his hand to his mouth and one by one he meticulously licked the sugar from the bun off his fingers. She swallowed a gasp as her body clenched and then sighed in delight. The memory of how he tasted was burned on her brain—spicy with a hint of citrus zip. And hot. Oh-so-flaming hot.

I thought the kiss never happened so why are we doing this?

She cleared her throat. 'I best go and write up the medication changes.'

'Bailey can do that.'

'Excuse me?'

He pushed off the bench. 'Get Bailey to do the medication changes and chase up the test results. I've got some far more interesting work for you.'

A skitter of excitement whipped through her. There'd been a rumour going around that a charity in India was making overtures to the castle in regards to separating a set of conjoined twins. Being part of the multidisciplinary team from the planning stages through to the massive operation and postoperative care would be the chance of a lifetime.

'Oh?' she said, far more casually than she felt.

'We're giving a paper at the spring symposium.'

A streak of surprise was followed by a trickle of dread. 'We?' She hated that it came out on a squeak.

He nodded. 'It's the tradition across all the medical departments that the specialist registrar in his or her last year of their fellowship always gives a joint presentation with their consultant.' He scratched his head and his brow furrowed. 'Did I not mention this to you when you first arrived?'

No! 'You did not,' she said, trying to sound calm. The dread was now spinning her stomach and sending out wave upon wave of nausea. 'This is the first I've heard of it.'

'Oh, well, not to worry,' he said with a grin that held a modicum of contrition. 'Lucky it's quiet so we should meet tomorrow's deadline.'

'Tomorrow.' Her screech of disbelief could

have given a sulphur-crested cockatoo a run for its money. 'But the symposium's still weeks away.'

'The papers are due tomorrow. The admin staff need time to print and bind them and prepare the handouts for the attendees.'

'We can't write a paper in a day.' She hated the squeak in her voice.

'Of course we can,' he said with all the easy confidence of someone who'd never had to think twice about reading or writing. 'Some of the best papers I've ever written have happened at that adrenaline-fuelled last-minute deadline.' Memories filled his handsome face. 'It's such a buzz to pull an all-nighter and finish as the fingers of dawn are lighting up the city.'

The very idea made her gag. 'That's not the way I work,' she countered, desperately clutching at straws. 'I mean, we don't even have a topic.'

'Of course we've got a topic,' he said, sounding amused. 'I wouldn't do that to you.'

'I guess I should be thankful for small mercies,' she said sarcastically.

'I'm sorry it slipped my mind, Claire. Your predecessor, Harry Banks, was supposed to write the paper, but as you know, he left us the moment things started looking rocky for the castle.' His face filled with kindness. 'I'm aware you like things to be ordered and just so, but believe me, stepping out of your comfort zone every now and then makes you feel alive.'

Oh. My. God. He was serious. He honestly thought he was doing her a favour. Her heart thumped so hard she was sure he must hear it. 'What's the topic?' she asked weakly.

His face lit up. 'Epilepsy surgery's the most effective way to control seizures in patients with drug-resistant focal epilepsy. I've got all the data. It's just a matter of assembling it and stringing it together with some well-chosen case studies. Don't panic. Most people prefer to attend the summer symposium on the Continent. The spring one's the smallest of the three. Think of it as a test run. If the paper's well received there, we can work it up into something bigger for *The Lancet*. Too easy.' He laughed. 'Isn't that what you Aussie's like to say?'

'Something like that,' she said faintly. The task he was asking her to undertake would be a significant one for most people, but for her the short time frame made it monumentally huge. Hopefully, she could find a quiet corner in the library where she could spread out the data and work her way through it slowly and methodically. 'I guess I better make a start, then.'

'Excellent.' He gave her warm smile. 'Give me fifteen minutes to grab a quick shower and then meet me in my office.'

No, no, no! Working alongside Alistair risked exposing her secret and she'd do anything to prevent that from happening. With a decisive movement that said *all business*, she pushed her glasses up her nose. 'I'll work in the library.'

He tilted his head and gave her a long and questioning look. Somehow, despite feeling like a desert plant wilting under the intense scrutiny of summer noontime heat, she managed to hold his gaze.

'It makes far more sense to work in my office,' he said, breaking the long silence. 'All the data's on my computer and there'll be far fewer interruptions and distractions there.'

Fewer distractions? She stifled a groan. Her much-needed day of physical distance from Alistair North had just imploded and sucked her down with it. Now, she faced spending the working day with him in the close confines of his office. Every breath she took would carry his musky scent. The air around her would vibrate with his bounding energy and any inadvertent brush of shoulders or hands, which invariably happened when two people worked in close proximity, would only serve to remind her how amazing the strength of his toned muscles and the tautness of his skin had felt last night under her hands.

All of it was one enormous distraction, but in

relative terms, her irrational attraction was the least of her worries. Her biggest problem was the challenge of hiding the fact she found data analysis and large writing tasks difficult. Under extreme pressure, it was almost impossible. If her boss discovered that, it could jeopardise her scholarship. She swallowed hard. There was only one solution—she had to get creative and make sure he never discovered her secret.

CHAPTER SIX

ALISTAIR STRODE ALONG Praed Street carrying a plastic bag containing take-away containers of Tandoori Chicken, Rogan Josh, curried vegetables and naan bread. The pungent aromas of the food made his stomach juices run and he picked up the pace. So much for a quiet day—he hadn't even managed lunch and he couldn't wait to tuck into the spicy delights.

It was eight in the evening and he'd been away from the office for hours. He hadn't intended for that to happen. In fact, when Dominic MacBride had telephoned at ten interrupting his writing day, he'd told him that a policy and procedures meeting didn't come under the banner of life or death. Today that was the only criteria that would get him to leave the office.

It was Claire who'd insisted he attend the meeting and raise the issue of referral waiting times. All had been dangerously pushed out since the staffing levels at the hospital had been decimated.

'The board needs to know their current actions are risking lives. I'd go but they won't listen to me. You've got FRCS after your name so surely that gives you more clout.'

'I doubt they can see past the dollar signs,' he'd said with a sigh, 'but you're right. It's worth a shot.'

He and Dominic had spent a frustrating few hours getting nowhere with the board and he'd been on his way back to the office when Morag called. 'Sorry, Alistair, but the Walkers are asking to see you. They're insisting upon it.'

He'd gone direct to ICU and the afternoon had rolled away from him as he'd dealt with a variety of issues. Truth be told, he should have called Bailey in to deal with most of them as they came under the banner of house officer jobs, but he'd been feeling generous. He could still remember how fraught life was as a junior doctor so he'd reinserted a central line and performed a lumbar puncture. He'd rather enjoyed the hands-on medicine, although that hadn't prevented a slight flicker of guilt that his largesse was a form of procrastination. As much as he disliked statistics, he knew he should be back in the office helping Claire with the difficult job instead of leaving her on her own to deal with it.

Given how horrified she'd both looked and sounded when she'd learned about the project, he'd been expecting to hear the return of her clipped and critical tones along with a lecture on time management each time he'd called her to notify her of yet another delay. However, on all three occasions all she'd said was, 'No worries. These things happen. Things are going well at this end.'

Ten minutes ago, just as he'd been paying for what he'd planned to be their dinner, she'd sent him a text.

No need to return to the office. Job done. Enjoy your evening.

He'd read it twice, trying to absorb the surprising and oddly dismaying text. He couldn't believe she'd finished the paper so quickly and without his help. Then again, he supposed if anyone was capable of knocking out something so complicated in a short space of time, it was probably Claire Mitchell. He'd tried to shrug off the unreasonable level of disappointment that they wouldn't be having dinner together. He'd been looking forward to returning to the office, sharing a curry, working on the paper and proving to her they were both adults and capable of being in the same room together without kissing each other.

No need for that. You've already done it.

He'd spent a restless night lurching between reliving the amazing and mind-blowing kiss and the unsettling feelings that stirred inside him whenever he recalled Claire's utterly appalled and slightly panicked post-kiss expression. As a result, he'd done his very British best at the interview with the Walkers last night and again this morning to sweep last night under the carpet and show Claire that everything was as it had been prior to the kiss. On one level he knew he should be pleased and relived that she regretted the incident. After all, they worked closely together and a fling wasn't conducive to workplace harmony, not to mention the fact it would break a dozen hospital rules. But then again, he wasn't used to anyone looking at him with such abhorrence. He felt a crazy need to prove to her that he was more than capable of respecting her wishes on the *nothing happened* front even though something incredible had taken place. He still couldn't reconcile the fact that prickly, terse Claire Mitchell could kiss a man better than his wildest fantasy.

He gave a wave to the evening protestors who were warming themselves around a brazier and then switched the take-away food bag to his other hand. For a brief moment he toyed with the idea of texting Islay Kennedy and inviting her to share the curries, but then his stomach growled. Hell, he was famished and he didn't want to delay. Taking the lift to level five, he punched in the security numbers and entered the consulting suite. After six each evening the lighting reverted to power-saving mode and the corridor was low-lit. He walked past a series of closed doors—the offices of his colleagues—and stopped in front of his, surprised by the spill of light coming from under the door. He turned the handle and stepped inside.

Holy— The first thing he saw was Claire Mitchell's sweet behind. She was leaning over his desk and the soft fabric of her dress fell in such a way that it perfectly outlined the two orbs of her cheeks. The memory of those curves pressed hard into his lap last night sent a raft of delicious sensation thrumming through him, heating his blood and making his palms itch. All he wanted to do was walk up behind her, pull her back into him and feel her pressing against hard him.

Good God! What the hell was wrong with him? This wasn't a role-play fantasy with a consenting partner. He was at work. She was his trainee and all of his thoughts were utterly inappropriate. He closed his eyes for a moment, concentrating hard on reducing his breathing from ragged to normal.

When he opened his eyes he avoided looking at the kryptonite that was her behind. Instead, he noticed her bare left foot was flat on the floor, her right knee was pressed into the seat of a chair and she was leaning over his desk. Her sun-gold hair had fallen free of its usual black band, cascading in shimmering waves across her shoulders. She held her arms outstretched in front of her, taking her weight on the heels of both hands, and her glasses dangled from the fingers of her left hand.

As his gaze strayed from her glasses, he noticed the paper. Papers to be exact. His entire office looked like someone had placed a fan in front of a ream of white A4 and turned it on full tilt. Pages spilled from the desk to the floor, some were stuck to the wall and others had migrated to his other desk and completely covered the green-tooled leather. Each page was filled with some sort of black printing—from graphs and tables to double-spaced words.

'Did it snow paper while I was gone?' he quipped as he quietly closed the door.

Claire swung around, shock etched deeply on her face and her colour as white as the paper. 'What are you doing here?'

'It's my office,' he said equably as he set down the take-away bag. 'More to the point, why are you here? You sent me a text saying you were finished.'

Her chin rose—a sure sign she was on the back foot. 'I thought I was done but I got caught up with a bit of tweaking.'

He snorted and swept his arm out to encompass the room. 'Tweaking? This looks like you're stuck smack bang in the mud-sucking middle.'

Something akin to panic crossed her face. 'And if I am?'

'It's exactly where I expected you to be.'

For a moment, her body went deathly still and then she abruptly shoved her glasses back on her face. 'You know?' she demanded in a voice that was half accusative and half defeated.

Know?

Then, as if someone had just poked her hard between her scapulas, her shoulders rolled back into a straight, sharp line and her nostrils flared. 'So this was deliberate? Some sort of macabre joke? Or worse? Sophisticated bullying to get back at me for last night? To put me in my place?'

Bullying? What the— He held up his hands as if a gun was being pointed menacingly at his head. 'Hang on just one damn minute, Dr Mitchell. That's a very serious accusation.'

She swept an arm through a pile of papers, sending them fluttering to the floor. 'And this is a serious setup. I can't believe how badly you want me to fail.'

Fail? His temper surged at her abhorrent claims. Every part of him screamed to carpet her here and now for insubordination and character assassination, but something about the tension pulling sharply at her features and the desolation in her eyes quelled his anger. The furious boil reduced to a slow and cross simmer. Once again he'd glimpsed those same malignant shadows clinging tightly where they didn't belong.

He sighed and dropped his arms, letting them fall loosely to his sides. 'Something's clearly upset you to make you behave like this but I'm at a loss as to what it is. When I said you were in the mud-sucking middle, I was referring to that moment in a project everyone experiences when you're suffering from information overload.'

She stared at him from behind her tortoiseshell glasses, intently studying his face. It was like she was trying to decode his words and match them up with his expression and tone of voice. He pressed on. 'That place in a project that demands you commence putting the data into a coherent form but the precise place to start eludes you.'

He tried for a wry smile. 'To be honest, I was very surprised to get your text saying you were finished. I expected you to only just be starting the narrative.'

For a moment she made no sound and then her face crumpled and a long, low moan escaped across her ruby-red lips. She sank onto the chair and dropped her face into her hands. 'Oh, God. No.'

The ragged sound carried old pain and it echoed around the quiet office before returning to cloak her in a toxic cloud. More than anything he wanted to reach out and touch her but then he remembered what had happened the last time he'd offered comfort. He decided that discretion was the better part of valour. He'd feed her instead.

As he silently dished up the food, she mumbled something, but given her faint volume, he assumed she was talking to herself rather than to him. Handing her a bowl of curry and some naan bread, he said, 'Want to tell me what's going on?'

Her hand shook as she accepted the bowl. 'Not really, no.'

'Put it this way. I was being polite.' He pulled up a chair and seated himself opposite her. 'You don't have an option.'

With a jerky movement, she set the bowl down on the desk. 'I can't eat knowing you're about to revoke my scholarship. Just do it and get it over with.'

He felt like he was watching a play where he'd missed act one and he was now totally muddled in act two. 'I haven't any intention of revoking your scholarship, although God knows why not, Claire Mitchell. Ever since you arrived, you've pushed the envelope and all of my buttons. You are by far *the* most challenging trainee I've ever worked with.'

She sucked in her lips. 'I… You…' She sighed and her head dropped. 'Sorry.'

It was the first time one of her apologies actually sounded sincere. Looking at the top of her bent head, he was still at a loss as to what was going on. 'I'm not sure you realise that you're also the most talented trainee I've ever had the fortune to work with.'

Her head rose slowly but her distinctive chocolate-brown brows had drawn down into a frown of doubt and anxiety. Yet again he was convinced she didn't come close to believing him. Exactly why, he had no idea. Nor did he understand why she was so convinced he'd been acting against her best interests. That accusation burned hot and cut deeply. In his private life he'd had women hurl accusations at him ranging from *commitment-phobe* to *heartless*, but at work he prided himself on equality and fairness. No one had ever suggested otherwise.

Looking for clues, he wracked his brain and tried to think of something he may have done or said to give her that impression. As he drew a blank, the mumbled words she'd spoken earlier suddenly sounded in his head as clear as a bell on a windless day.

Everything's falling apart just as I always knew it would.

Why, with a track record of successes, did his most talented trainee believe she was going to fail? He'd bet his last pound that whatever or whoever had caused those tormenting shadows of hers was connected to this eroding self-belief. He was determined to find the source.

'If we're to continue working together, Claire, I need to know two things. Why you texted me saying you were finished when obviously you are nowhere near, and more importantly, why you would even entertain the thought I had set you up to fail?'

From the moment Alistair had stepped into the office, Claire's heart had picked up its pace and now it was beating so quickly and erratically that she was light-headed and dizzy. She still couldn't wrap her head around how rapidly things had unravelled. Not that she'd ever been in control of the project, but she'd been convinced she was in control of keeping Alistair far, far away from the office for the bulk of the day. Except now he was here and she was backed into a corner of her own making. The only available escape route was ripping out her soul.

His words *'You're exactly where I expected you to be'* had not only left her feeling utterly exposed, they'd hauled her backwards into the dark abyss that was her school days in Gundiwindi. She hated the emotions the past always generated. When she'd combined them with her determination that no one was ever going to bully her again, she'd lashed out, only to discover Alistair had no idea about her secret. No one got away with incorrectly accusing their boss of a heinous crime without having to face the consequences. This was her Armageddon.

Everything she'd worked so hard to achieve was about to shatter into a thousand irreparable pieces and she only had herself to blame. Lacing her fingers together tightly, she fixed her gaze on the tip of his left ear. 'I'm—' she forced the word up and out through a tight throat '—dyslexic.'

He looked utterly taken aback. 'Are you sure?' Doubt rang in his very precise accent.

'Your daughter's not going to amount to very much, Mr Mitchell.'

'Moron.'

'You're a very lazy girl. Accept that you belong in the remedial class.'

'Dumb ass.'

Against the harsh memories of the past, a bark of laughter fully loaded with derision broke out of her, raining down on them both. 'Oh, believe me. I'm more than sure. Dyslexia's been my constant companion since I started primary school.'

'But...'

Confusion shone in his eyes. A part of her wanted to hug him that he'd been clueless about her condition. The rest of her ached with embarrassment that she'd got herself into the situation where she was forced to tell him.

'I don't understand,' he finally managed to say as he ran a hand through his hair, making it even messier than usual. 'If you have this disability, how on earth have you got this far in your career?'

She shrugged. 'Sheer bloody-mindedness and a photographic memory.'

This time he laughed—a great booming sound that twirled around her with reassuring gravitas. 'Well, you do have bloody-mindedness in spades.'

She smiled weakly. 'Um, thank you, I guess.' She didn't know what else to say.

'Determination can carry a person a very long way.'

Unwanted tears pricked at the back of her eyes and she blinked furiously, refusing to allow them to form, let alone fall. 'When you're told often enough that you're useless, it can go one of two ways.'

Respect flared on his face. 'And you chose success.'

She thought of her years of struggle and for the first time she glimpsed what she'd achieved in a new light. 'I suppose I have.'

'I'd say you definitely have.' He gave her a contemplative glance. 'Why didn't you tell me about the dyslexia?'

She tossed her head. 'I refuse to be defined by it.'

'But you are.'

His words crashed into her, making her chest cramp in twisting pain. She'd spent years proving she was no different from anyone else and she wasn't about to accept his view. 'No. I. Am. Not. You said yourself you had no idea I was dyslexic.'

'That's not what I'm talking about. All of us are an amalgam of our experiences.' The skin on his bladed cheeks momentarily tensed and then relaxed. 'You live with a learning disability. I imagine that isn't always easy.'

'No,' she said softly, appreciating his insight on that point if not on the other.

'Exactly how hard is it? Was it?'

The question made her flinch. 'I don't waste time thinking about it.'

Although a flash of sympathy lit up his eyes, his mouth straightened into a taut line. 'Perhaps not consciously, but I think it all came out to play today when you accused me of bullying.'

The sternness of his voice didn't hide his hurt and it ate into her. 'I'm sorry. I should never—'

'I don't want an apology, Claire,' he interrupted briskly. 'But I require an explanation as to why you would make that leap.'

She knew she owed him the truth but that didn't stop her feeling as if she was about to rip herself open from the inside out. *Just do it and get it over with.* 'I grew up in a tiny outback town where sport ruled and there was no tolerance for being different. Not only was I myopic, I struggled to learn, which made me a sitting duck for cruel kids.'

'Bullies?'

'Yep.' A long sigh shuddered out of her. 'Although, in retrospect, it wasn't the kids who were the worst offenders. I had an ally in my brother, who was a well-respected football player. He stomped on anyone who stole my glasses and pinched my books. By the time I left primary school, I had amassed a lot of one-liners. A clever putdown confused most of the boys who were all brawn and no brains.'

'I can imagine,' he said with a knowing smile. 'I can see where you honed your acerbic skills.'

Her cheeks burned with embarrassed heat as her mind spun with confusion. She'd been so rude to him and yet here he was actively listening and trying to understand. As much as she disliked talking about her life prior to university, she wanted to honour his interest and hopefully hold on to her job.

'The saying "Everything's there but it's wired differently" is my brain. Spelling and reading have always been a challenge. I had trouble linking the sound of a word to the letters on the page.

When I was little, there was no reading recovery program and as the years went past I slipped further and further behind.

'I was accused of being lazy and not putting in the effort. Teachers took to saying, "You're nothing like your brother," and it was easier for them to label me the difficult child. Mum and Dad tried to help but as I was frustrating qualified teachers, it wasn't surprising that my parents eventually accepted what they'd been told. Eyes were constantly rolled in class when I struggled to read out loud and I never gained my pen licence. By the end of primary school, nothing was expected of me. Everyone assumed the moment I turned fifteen, I'd leave school.'

His leaned forward slightly. 'What changed?'

'A guardian angel called Strez.' She smiled and gave a self-deprecating laugh. 'Mr Strezinski. He was a Polish migrant who spoke four languages. I have no idea how he landed up at Gundiwindi High or why he agreed to teach typing and woodwork. Fortunately for me, I took both subjects. He saw something in me no one else did. He lent me audiobooks so I could hear the English texts while I read along. Without having to agonise over every word, I could hear the themes and analyse the text. He suggested I type my assignments.'

Her heart swelled as it did whenever she

thought of Strez. 'I'll never forget the day I got a B+ on an essay. I was both over the moon about the mark and white with fury that I had to prove to the teacher I hadn't plagiarised the work. Strez helped me devise strategies, like chewing gum, to help me focus and using headphones to block out extraneous noise. Most importantly, he was the one person who truly believed in me.'

Alistair nodded and a lock of hair fell forward. He brushed it aside. 'He sounds like a true mentor.'

She looked up into his eyes, which in the low light were the colour of silver moonbeams dancing on water. 'He changed my life. Without his help, I'd never have passed Year Twelve, let alone got into medicine. He released me from all of Gundiwindi's preconceived ideas.'

His brow's rose questioningly. 'But not, I think, from its legacy.'

She considered the statement. 'I've never thought about it in those terms. You may have a point.'

This time he gave a bark of laughter. 'There's no *may*, Claire. I see it in your eyes. There's a part of you that still believes you're that struggling little girl.'

'That's because I am.' The words shot out before she could catch them back. *Idiot!* She hated feeling so vulnerable in front of him. 'You're the first person outside of Gundiwindi to know I'm dyslexic. I only told you to try and save my job.'

A sympathetic look similar to the one he'd shown her last night flashed across his face. For a moment she yearned for a touch of his hand and immediately thought better of it. She couldn't trust herself not to lean in and repeat last night's kiss, and *that* was totally out of the question.

He moved abruptly, picking up her curry from the desk and pressing it on her. 'Eat this before it goes cold.'

She gratefully accepted it, having discovered that not being fired on the spot had revived her appetite. She was suddenly ravenous. Using the garlic naan, she scooped up some curry and savoured the subtle flavours.

'Part of me can understand why you've kept it quiet,' Alistair said. 'Medicine's fiercely competitive with a take-no-prisoners approach.'

'And I learned that hard lesson in the Gundiwindi playground. Never expose a weakness or you get trampled. Like anyone with a secret, I've gone to great lengths and become very good at hiding it. Today was no exception.' She huffed out a breath and looked him straight in the eye. 'I didn't want you here working alongside me. I couldn't risk you seeing how I have to read things twice to decipher them and once more to memorise them.'

His high forehead creased into deep lines. 'So that's why you told me you'd completed the job. You wanted to keep me away.'

She nodded and he added drily, 'Well, that answers my question as to why you were so unexpectedly conciliatory about my extended absence today.'

She gave an apologetic shrug. 'When you arrived back here and said you expected me to be in the mud-sucking middle, I thought you'd deliberately given me this task to expose my biggest weakness and my worst fear.'

Understanding rolled across his face. Ruefulness followed immediately, settling in the lines around his mouth and eyes. 'My general dislike of statistics combined with my procrastination became your worst nightmare.'

'The project isn't the nightmare.' She hurried to reassure him. 'It's the short timeline.'

He helped himself to more Tandoori Chicken. 'So what I've interpreted as officious organisation is in fact one of your coping strategies?'

She nodded slowly. 'I need time to read and memorise. I can't leave anything to the last minute.'

'And I leave everything to the last minute.'

'Why is that when it must make things more difficult for you?' she asked, genuinely interested.

A muscle in his cheek twitched unexpectedly.

'Because life's far too short to spend so much time doing stuff I don't enjoy.'

And there it was again—his selfish streak. A strand of disappointment wound through her with more intensity than she cared to experience. What did it matter to her if he was a fully paid up and card carrying member of the *live for today and for me* club.

'The first thing I did when I qualified was activate the fine tradition of all consultants and dump the bulk of the boring paperwork onto my trainees.' He suddenly winced and rubbed the back of his neck. 'Hell, Claire. No wonder we've been crossing swords. I've exhausted you.'

Guilt slugged her. 'I should have told you I was struggling, but now you know why I didn't.' She gave him an apologetic shrug. 'All of the above. The thing is, in my previous positions I've never had to deal with quite so much paperwork. Brain surgery is so much easier than reading and writing. As for public speaking, I fear death less.'

He laughed. 'Dyslexia aside, you're not alone there.' His expression sobered. 'Despite—or perhaps because of—your dyslexia and the type of brain you have, you're an excellent neurosurgeon.'

Gratitude flowed through her and for the first time she actually accepted and believed in the compliment. 'Thank you. Surgery's spatial and kinaesthetic learning.'

'The practical component is, but what about all those years of lectures?'

'Like I said, I have a visual memory. Just don't ask me to write anything quickly or my *"p"*'s will become *"b"*'s and vice versa, along with a lot of other words spelt backwards. Oh, and never get me to navigate because I can't follow a map, and don't expect me to identify left or right without making my left hand into an *L*.'

He grinned. 'I'll remember that.'

She watched his open and friendly face and saw kindness reflected there. Other consultants would have summoned security to march her off the premises for her earlier behaviour. Although she'd hardly enjoyed his insistence she tell him about her dyslexia and school days in Gundiwindi, she appreciated it because it had saved her job. Sure, the man had a selfish side but how could she have ever thought he was shallow? Or that he wanted her to fail?

'Claire, I meant what I said about you being best trainee I've ever had. I can teach you and make you even better, but if we're going to make this work, we need to be a team. We need to be on the same page.'

Her heart added a beat. 'I came close to throwing away my chance, didn't I?'

'Put it this way. You're lucky you're so talented and that I'm so easy-going.' He gave her a wink as he set down his now empty bowl, wiped clean with the bread. His face settled into serious lines. 'Is there anything else you're finding difficult about working with me?'

Her mouthful of curry stalled mid-swallow as their shared kiss flashed like a neon light in her mind.

He means aside from the fact your body goes on hyper-alert whenever you think about him. Aside from the fact you kissed him senseless.

She cleared her throat. 'Ah, no. Um, well, not that I can think of right at the moment.'

His eyes did that intense staring thing that made her feel as if he could see down to her soul. 'Are you sure?'

'Absolutely,' she said, trying to sound cool, calm and detached instead of a quivering mess of liquid lust. 'But I give you my word that I'll discuss any problems with you if and when they arise.'

A wide and reassuring smile broke across his face and she saw immediately why his little patients and their parents trusted him implicitly. Almost everything she'd ever believed about Alistair North had just been turned on its head.

'I'm glad we've had this conversation. It's important we're on the same page and it's going to make the ball a much more enjoyable evening.'

The ball. Her stomach flipped. So much had

changed between them since she'd insisted he attend the ball and he'd turned the tables on her by buying her ticket. Thank goodness she'd already told Victoria to seat her on the opposite side of the ten-seat table from Alistair. The width of the table meant conversation between them would be impossible.

Seriously? You're worried about conversation? Be worried about the close proximity of a bloke who will rock a tux.

'Indeed,' she somehow managed to say and sound professional.

'Excellent. Consider this conversation your first staff assessment, which, by the way, you've passed. I'll get around to writing up your report, but first, I have a paper to write before nine tomorrow morning.'

An hour ago she'd have been tempted to take a crack at the chaos his procrastination had caused him, but given how generous he'd been to her that would be grossly unfair.

He scratched his head and blew out a sigh as he took in the sea of papers. 'Where to start exactly,' he said quietly as if he was thinking out loud.

As wonderful as the idea of sleep was, she'd have to be blind not to notice the dark rings under his eyes. She didn't have a monopoly on a sleep debt and to walk away now and leave him dealing with the project after he'd just gone beyond what was expected of an understanding boss wasn't something she could do.

'To the uninitiated it looks like a mess but I promise you there's a system.'

'I believe you, but thousands wouldn't,' he said with a laugh in his voice. 'Were you able to draw any conclusions from the data?'

'I was.'

'Thank goodness.'

This time she laughed. 'I'll tell you what I discovered, if you convert it into flowing words that are spelt correctly.'

'You're on.' He opened up a new document on his computer. 'And there's a silver lining to all of this, Claire.'

'There is?'

'Sure.' He gave her a bone-melting smile. 'At the end of a long night, we'll be rewarded with a perfect view of dawn breaking over London.'

She tried not to think about the fact that she had a perfect view in front of her right this minute.

CHAPTER SEVEN

LONDON HAD PUT on a warm, starlit evening for the Paddington Children's Hospital fundraising ball and from the balcony overlooking the Thames the scent of gardenias wafted on the air. The evening was in full swing—the dance floor was crowded, some potential couples seeking a quiet tête-à-tête lingered on the curve of the elegant art nouveau staircase and the liveried staff busily cleared away the remnants of the main course.

The opulence and grandeur of the nineteenth century Paris salon–styled ballroom was equally matched by the massive floral arrangements of white roses, gardenias and hydrangeas as well as by the crowd. Alistair was used to seeing his staff in their PCH uniform or scrubs. He was used to seeing Claire in her utilitarian white blouse, black skirt, white coat and with her hair pulled back in a ponytail. He sure as hell wasn't used to seeing her in a full-length ball gown with her hair piled up onto her head in a way that emphasised her long and slender neck. A neck that just screamed to be kissed.

Many of the women wore strapless dresses exposing acres of skin and generous cleavages that drew and glued the gazes of most of the men in the room. Usually, he'd have enjoyed the spectacle—hell, he'd probably have toyed with the idea of later in the evening burying his face deep into their pillow softness—but not tonight. Somehow, Claire, in her high-necked sleeveless gown with its beaded bodice and full skirt, was sexier than all of them put together. The combination was doing his head in and the irony of the evening wasn't lost on him either.

Two weeks ago when he'd insisted on bringing Claire to the ball it had been a personal challenge to see if the buttoned-up woman with the acerbic tongue was capable of enjoying herself. Back then his plan had been to crack her façade, get her to smile and, as her boss, show her that there was more to life than just work. Fate, however, had thumbed its nose at him again.

Of all people, he knew better than most how life could change in a heartbeat. Or, in his case, a lack of one. With that information etched onto his heart and soul it stood to reason that he should have anticipated how much could happen in two weeks. He had not. Tonight, he was faced with the reality of change.

For starters, there'd been *that* kiss neither of them was acknowledging and then they'd had their frank conversation in his office. Since that night, the stressed-out and snarky woman he'd thought was Claire had almost vanished. Tonight, in her place, was a woman he barely recognised inside or out.

Since he'd learned about her dyslexia and they'd pulled a companionable and constructive all-nighter on the paper for the symposium, the two of them had reset their working relationship. Now that he understood her struggles with the written word, he'd taken back the lion's share of the report writing, leaving her with an amount she assured him she could handle. With more sleep, the dead weight of hiding a secret being lifted and a workload she could manage, Claire Mitchell's general demeanour had softened. In the last fourteen days, without even trying, his professional respect for her work and his admiration for what she'd achieved against steep odds had tipped the scales. He liked her.

That's not a crime, he told himself before his subconscious could berate him. *I liked her predecessor, Harry, too.*

But you didn't kiss him.

He had no comeback to that. All he knew was that if Claire was going to the same lengths as he was not to act on the wide current of attraction that arced between them every time they stepped into each other's orbit, then she was well down the road to insanity. This thing between them lived and breathed. It flickered and flared like firelight and it tantalisingly danced and sparkled like sunshine on water. No matter how hard he tried to ignore its pull, it never completely disappeared. It was playing merry hell with his concentration.

When he was alone, his thoughts were full of her and when they were together at work he was like a cat on a hot tin roof. Simple things like the brush of fingers on his hand when he passed her a pen or when he accepted her offer of a cup of coffee took on cataclysmic proportions. Any inadvertent touch set off rafts of sensation that tumbled over and over each other, racing along his veins until he was on fire with a thirst for her that couldn't be slaked. His body, which craved release, ranted at him all the time to *just do it.*

It took more willpower than he'd ever imposed upon himself before not to throw caution to the wind, spin her into his arms and kiss her senseless. Hell, just the other day during surgery she'd reached over him and to avoid an inadvertent touch he'd pulled back so fast that he'd upended a tray of sterilised instruments. The scrub sister was yet to forgive him.

He wasn't used to holding back. Hell, what was

the point when the future couldn't be predicted and any day may well be his last. He'd always acted on intoxicating zips of attraction between him and a woman. If Claire had been any other woman and she'd kissed him with that same intense abandon, he knew without a doubt they'd have spent the rest of the night burning up the sheets. Instead, they'd shared the oddest fortnight, lurching from strict professional courtesy to relaxed moments of friendship. All the while the unacknowledged attraction simmered so strongly between them that he didn't know if he was coming or going. Tonight was no exception.

'Oh. Hello,' Claire said with a friendly—if slightly hesitant—smile as she passed him walking back from the dance floor.

Strands of her golden-blonde hair had escaped from the pile atop her head, her cheeks were flushed pink and her contact-lens-covered caramel eyes were almost obliterated by her dilated ebony pupils. She looked like she'd just been tumbled onto her back and ravished. His blood dived to his groin and he grabbed a glass of water from a passing waiter, drinking it down fast to stifle a groan.

'It's warm, isn't it?' She took a proffered glass of water too. 'I've danced with Dominic and Matthew but thank goodness I only have to dance with Andrew once. My toes couldn't take much more.'

'Hmm,' he managed, frantically channelling thoughts of the icy cold streams in the Scottish Highlands where his father had started teaching him to fly-fish. Thoughts about the effect the chilly water always had on his body.

Although he'd paid for her ticket to the ball, he hadn't spent very much time with her this evening, which was both a good and a bad thing. She'd refused his offer to pick her up and drive her, insisting instead on meeting him here. When he'd arrived, he'd looked for her but he'd soon been absorbed into a group so by the time he reached their allocated table and discovered that Victoria had seated them on opposite sides of the large round, it was too late to do anything about it.

He'd spent the entrée and main course flanked on one side by a chatty physiotherapist and on the other side by the ward pharmacist. Both were perfectly delightful and interesting women and on another night he'd have probably enjoyed their company immensely. But tonight, every time he'd heard Claire's tinkling laugh—yes, the woman had actually laughed—he'd wanted to lunge across the table and throttle Duncan MacKinnon.

If anyone was going to make Claire laugh, it was going to be him. If anyone was going to show her how to have fun, it should be him, except he hadn't had the chance. The moment the meal had finished, the dancing had started and Victoria had sold him off like he was meat on a slab. He'd danced for an hour straight, fending off a dozen invitations from sexy and beautiful women. It both surprised and worried him that he hadn't been tempted by any of them. What the hell was wrong with him?

You know exactly what's wrong with you. Ethics and blue balls.

'Does Victoria know you're hiding behind the aspidistra instead of being out on the dance floor?' Claire asked with a teasing glint in her beautiful eyes.

This time he gulped champagne. From the moment he'd first laid eyes on her tonight, he'd recognised that off-duty Claire was a very different woman from Dr Mitchell. Out from under the mantle of responsibility and the pressures of her dyslexia, the need for her to control everything had faded. If anything, tonight she had a look of wonder about her, as if she couldn't quite believe she was at the ball and she was absorbing every moment. None of it was helping him control his libido in any shape or form.

'I'm not hiding. I'm taking a break.'

She laughed. 'Poor, Al. What a tough gig, having beautiful women throw themselves at you.'

Al? 'You have no idea,' he said tightly, thinking about the battle that currently raged inside him. The beautiful woman he wanted wasn't throwing herself at him, and unless she did, he couldn't have her.

Lighten up, mate. Forcing himself to smile just like he'd been doing all evening, he said, 'But one must do one's bit to help save the castle.'

'You Brits break me up,' she said, laughing. 'Keep calm and dance on?'

'Something like that,' he said, thinking that he hadn't known calm since he'd kissed her.

'Victoria, Rosie, Matt and Robyn have done an amazing job pulling this together. Apparently, their photo's going to be in the paper tomorrow, so hopefully donations will flood in.' She gazed up at the ceiling with a starry-eyed look, taking in the intricate plasterwork and gilt. 'All of this is so far removed from the Gundiwindi Mechanic's Institute hall I keep thinking I'm dreaming it.' She swung her gaze to his. 'Did you know that Anna Pavlova once danced here and that Fred Astaire danced on the roof with his sister?'

He loved the awe that wove across her face and he had a crazy desire to try and keep it there and never let it fade. 'How do you know all this?'

'I stumbled across a photographic exhibition,' she said enthusiastically. 'Once, there was a leopard in this stunning Belle Époque room. Can you imagine?'

'Well, us crazy Brits like to shake things up a bit now and then,' he said with a grin.

'Alistair.' A voice with an Irish lilt called his name from the dance floor. A Cornish accent followed it. 'Come dance with us.'

'Yes, do,' a chorus of accents from around the British Isles sang across the ballroom.

The Koala Ward nurses were excelling at having fun, but the last thing he wanted was to be back in that pawing crush. He smiled at Claire. 'I wouldn't mind seeing those photos.'

'You're just saying that to avoid the tipsy nurses.'

Absolutely. 'As a Londoner, I think it's imperative I catch up on the history of this esteemed establishment.'

She gave an exaggerated eye roll and a lightness shot through him. 'Exactly where do I find this exhibition?'

'Downstairs. You cross the foyer, go left at reception, take the first right and there's a set of double doors—' She laughed. 'It's probably just easier if I show you.'

Yes, please. He stepped back, allowing her the space to move past him and then it was just good manners to rest his hand lightly on the small of her back to guide her as they negotiated their way across the crowded room.

'Alistair, old man,' Lionel Harrington, a retired paediatric surgeon, called out to him with a definite slur in his voice.

Claire slowed and Alistair leaned forward, saying quietly into her ear, 'Keep going or we'll be stuck with loquacious Lionel for the next half an hour.'

She immediately picked up the pace, walking determinedly against the crowd who were now returning for dessert. Instead of summoning a lift, she picked up her skirt and with a smoothness of motion that belied her high heels she almost sailed down the stunning staircase.

He had a flash of Cinderella running away from the Prince and he hurried down after her. He automatically turned towards the foyer but she grabbed his hand and pulled him through a door and down a corridor. It wasn't decorated in quite the same grand style as the rest of the hotel and he had a sudden thought. 'Are we allowed back here?'

Her hand paused on the door handle of a set of double doors and her eyes danced. 'Put it this way. There's no sign saying that we're not.'

He laughed, loving that she was living for the moment. She immediately shushed him. Using what he assumed was the staff entrance, he followed her into a large room. Large crates, ladders and other equipment were scattered around the room and half of the space was hung with framed photographs of various sizes.

He picked up a flyer that had spilled from a box. 'It says it opens on the fourth.'

'How lucky are we to get an advanced peek,' she said, eyes shining as she tugged him towards an enormous black and white photo. 'Ta-dah!'

He did a double take. 'Is that a five-foot cake balanced on an elephant that's standing on a gondola?'

'I know, right?' she said, laughter lacing her voice. Dropping her hand from his arm, she peered forward to read the information plaque next to the photo. 'And it says it was lit by four hundred paper lanterns.'

He had to fist his hand so as not to snatch hers back. 'I'm quite taken with the twelve thousand carnations and the swans.'

She shook her head in amazement. 'I can't even wrap my head around such extravagance.'

Side by side they wandered slowly up and down the room taking in the photos of famous people. Bogart and Bacall, and Marilyn Monroe, represented Hollywood royalty. There was a very young Christian Dior surrounded by five models dressed in intricately beaded ball gowns.

Personally, he didn't think any of them looked as amazing as Claire.

'Here's one for you,' he said, pointing to a portrait of the famous Australian soprano, Dame Nellie Melba. It was taken when she was young and she was pressing a fan coquettishly to her cheek. 'The hotel's chef invented peach Melba to honour her triumph at Covent Garden.'

Claire laughed. 'I bet it was far more extravagant than the Gundiwindi pub's best efforts of some canned cling peaches served with half-melted ice cream.'

'You forgot the raspberry sauce.'

'There's raspberry sauce in peach Melba?'

'Good heavens,' he said with faux shock. 'What sort of Australian are you if you don't know that?'

'Obviously a dessert-ignorant one. I guess I'll be forced to remedy the situation.'

He had a sudden flash of her mouth closing around a spoon and slowly sucking ice cream off it. He was abruptly very hot and finding it hard to breathe. Tugging at his collar, he loosened his bow tie.

One of the last photos in the collection was taken during the Second World War. 'I can't imagine dancing while the bombs fell,' Claire said softly.

He could. Dicing with death was a way of life

for him with his unreliable heart. 'Why not enjoy yourself to the very last?'

She gave him a sideways look. 'More of your live-for-the-moment mantra?'

'Sure. Just like we're living for the moment now.'

A small frown creased her forehead. 'I hardly think sneaking in here is very dangerous.'

'Oh, I don't know…'

She tilted her head, looking at him from those glorious eyes of hers. Her perfume, which always reminded him of sunshine, summer days and freedom, pulled at his restraint. So help him, he should have stayed upstairs and danced with the giggly nurses instead of coming down here with her. But here they were, alone for the very first time this evening, and all he wanted to do was wrap his arms around her. He wanted to haul her in against him, feel her body pressed against the length of him and lose himself in kissing her until nothing else existed but their touch.

You know you can't do any of it.

He never prevaricated or second-guessed anything but this was new territory for him. This was Claire and he was her boss. Until she gave him a sign that she felt exactly the same way he did, that she would welcome his touch, nothing could happen.

'How can this possibly be dangerous,' she said

briskly with a hint of the terse Claire from two weeks ago.

He knew her well enough to recognise the tone she used when she was stressed. Was it because she could feel this thing leaping and writhing between them, desperate to be satiated? *Please.* He gazed down at her and said softly, 'I think you know exactly how dangerous it is for us to be alone in this room.'

Alistair's impossibly deep voice flowed around Claire like dark, melted chocolate—decadent, enticing and blissfully sinful. She knew exactly how dangerous it was for her to be standing mere millimetres away from him and his rock-hard body. A body her fingertips had committed to memory just over two weeks ago and itched to touch again.

You had a plan. Why didn't you stick to it?

So much had happened between them since the evening she'd invited him to the ball and all of it made her head spin. Back when she'd issued the invitation, all he'd been to her was an infuriating and exasperating boss. Since then, she'd seen more sides to him than a polygon. When she combined it with *that* kiss, it made him—for her at least—the most dangerous man in London. It didn't matter how great he'd been about her slightly unhinged behaviour around the Walker case or his empathy and practicality about her dyslexia, or that she now recognised in him values and ethics that she admired. No matter how much her body ached to touch his again, they were still in the power dynamic of boss and trainee.

To that end, she'd gone to great lengths to protect herself from doing something she'd regret at work. Tonight, she'd had a simple and foolproof plan for the evening—never be alone with Alistair. She'd known that outside of the protective framework of the hospital and their defined roles she might be tempted, so she'd strategised for it. She'd started by politely refusing his offer of a ride to the hotel and until now she'd only talked to him in the ballroom surrounded by three hundred people.

Why in heaven's name had she brought him down here?

She blamed the dress and the hotel. Tonight was like stepping out of her prescribed life and into a magical world of pretend. It had started the moment she'd stared disbelievingly at the woman who'd faced her in the bedroom mirror. She'd hardly recognised herself. The boutique owner on a little road just off Oxford Street deserved a medal for convincing her to buy this frock. The little girl from dusty Gundiwindi had ridden to the ball in a London black cab, which in her book was as amazing as a pumpkin car-

riage being drawn by white horses. The moment
the hotel's doorman had swept open the cab's
door and she'd stepped onto the green carpet,
she'd been treated as if she was someone special.
Someone who mattered. That was her ambrosia.

The opulence and grandeur of the surroundings
had called to her and she'd been like a kid in a
lolly shop. She'd gone exploring, making her way
noiselessly along thickly carpeted corridors and
peeking behind closed doors. When she'd stumbled into the half-hung exhibition, she'd been so
excited about discovering the living history of the
luxurious hotel that she'd wanted to share it with
someone. It had totally messed with her plan. So
here she was, alone with Alistair, and although
his hands were by his sides and not a single cell
of their bodies touched, the electricity that buzzed
and fizzed between them could light up London
and the home counties.

For the first time, the look in his eyes was un-
guarded. The professional interest that usually
resided in the grey depths whenever he looked
at her—a glance that occasionally morphed into
moments of a friendly gaze—had vanished. In
its place, the flames of unadulterated lust burned
brightly. Danger and desire swirled with an intoxicating pull.

Her body responded to it, leaping with a need

to match his. Fleetingly, she wondered why he'd dropped his guard. Why now?

It's this hotel. This dress. This night. None of it's real life.

Exactly. So take what's on offer because it will vanish with the dawn.

She swallowed and dug to find her voice, not quite believing she could be so daring. 'You once accused me of not having fun. This hotel, with all of its stories, almost demands I step outside of my real life and do something outrageous for a night.'

His eyes flashed silver. 'It would almost be disrespectful not to honour the hotel's reputation as a host to many clandestine lovers.'

Tingling delight swooped through her and she was dizzy with the idea that he wanted her as much as she wanted him. But memories of Michael, along with a deep-seated need to protect herself and her scholarship, made her say, 'This has nothing to do with work. What happens in the hotel stays in the hotel.'

Tension coiled through his body, radiating from the jut of his jaw and out across the square set of his shoulders, but still he didn't move to touch her. 'I promise you, Claire. It won't spill into our work world. It's your decision. If you have any doubts...' His husky voice cracked. 'Are you absolutely certain you want this?'

Her heart rolled oddly at the concern in his

question and she plucked at the organza of her full skirt. After working with him for weeks she recognised him to be an honourable man. She trusted him and knew that he'd never coerce her or use this night against her. She met his gaze. 'Tonight's all about fantasy, right?'

He made a low growling sound in the back of his throat. It made her feel strangely powerful and she rose on her toes to kiss him. For two long weeks she'd replayed the juxtaposing touch of his mouth on hers—soft and firm—and the searing heat of his lips that lit her up from the inside out. She couldn't wait another second for his taste to invade her.

Knowing his mouth was millimetres from hers, she closed her eyes and leaned in. Her lips hit air. As disappointment whipped her, Alistair grabbed her hand. He pulled her so fast towards the double doors that she almost tripped. 'What are you doing?' she asked, frantically trying to keep her balance.

'What the hell do you think I'm doing?' He wrenched open the door.

'I thought you were going to kiss me.'

He stopped and gently cupped her cheeks, his palms warm against her skin. 'If I kiss you here, Claire,' he said raggedly, 'I won't be able to stop.'

The little girl inside her squealed, twirled and clapped her hands. 'Really?'

'Yes, really.' He dropped his forehead to gently rest against hers. 'I've wanted to kiss you from the moment I saw you across the other side of the crowded ballroom. I'm not ruining this fantasy of ours by getting charged with indecent exposure. We're getting a room.'

'But Marlene Dietrich apparently—'

But he was already towing her across the foyer towards the reception desk. With one arm clamped firmly around her waist, keeping her tightly pressed against him, he said in a crisp, polite and plummy voice, 'We'd like a room for the evening.'

The receptionist—his name badge said he was Daniel—didn't bat an eyelid. Nor did he ask about their luggage or lack of it. 'These functions can be quite exhausting, sir. I'm sure you'll find everything you need in Room 613.' After running Alistair's credit card through the machine he gave them a wallet containing two key cards. 'Just insert the card into the lift, sir, and press six. Enjoy your evening.'

At that precise moment Claire developed a fondness for what up until now she'd always considered starchy, British manners.

'Thank you,' Alistair said as he turned her and briskly marched them both to the lifts.

The journey to the sixth floor was interminable with the lift stopping at almost every floor.

Their slow progression added to her frustration that Alistair was holding firm to his resolve that he wasn't going to kiss her until they were inside the room. 'You're crushing my hand.'

'Sorry.' He gave her a tight and apologetic glance before dropping her hand and hitting the number six button another three times.

She used the tortoise-like passage of time to slip off her shoes. When the lift doors finally opened on their level she picked up her skirt and her shoes, stepped out into the corridor and ran. Just as she'd found their door, Alistair caught her around the waist with his left hand and with his right he inserted the card into the lock with a quick in-out action.

'You've done that before.'

'Never with quite the same level of desperation,' he said with an ironic edge. He pushed open the door.

Together, they tumbled into the room, and as the door clicked shut quietly behind them, he kissed her.

Unlike that first time in the lounge, there was nothing slow about this kiss. It held two weeks of frustration and tightly leashed lust that now spilled into her with an urgency that chased along her veins. As it scooped up her desire and merged it into a molten ball of need, it detonated bursts of wonder. The explosions lit her up until her body was a pleasure dome of sensation and her legs threatened to buckle out from under her.

In a sea of organza and tulle she fell back onto the king-size bed, bringing Alistair down with her. Her hands tugged at his bespoke jacket, pushing it off his shoulders, and as he shrugged out of it his mouth didn't leave hers. Somehow, despite the fact his kisses had reduced her body to a puddle of vibrating need and her mind to mush, she managed to get her fingers to work. She undid the buttons of his waistcoat and popped the studs on his shirt and collar. Finally, after clawing at a flurry of white material, her palms pressed against hot skin, corded tendon and rock-solid muscle. *Bliss.*

As she ran her hands across his chest she heard herself make an involuntary moan. Alistair pulled his mouth from hers and gazed down at her with a wide grin on his face. 'Having fun?'

Her cheeks burned and she reminded herself that as much as he wanted her for his own enjoyment, she wanted him. He was hers for this night and it would be silly to waste precious time by being embarrassed. 'You bet I'm having fun,' she said, lifting her head and laying her mouth over his left nipple. She flicked out her tongue, tasting the hard nub, and then she sucked him into her mouth.

He gasped and his entire body flinched.

'Vixen,' he muttered, and as she laughed his hands moved frantically across the bodice of her dress. She could barely feel his touch through the detailed beading and corsetry and her laugher faded. She wanted his hands on her skin. His mouth on her skin. She wanted—

'Bloody hell,' he said through gritted teeth. 'I'll get gravel rash from all this beadwork.'

'The zipper's on the—' She suddenly had a face full of organza and tulle, but before she could fight the material, Alistair's mouth nipped gently at the tender skin of her inner thigh.

'Oh.' She gasped and writhed in delight as his tongue flicked and his mouth sucked, all the while moving closer and closer to her hot and aching centre. Her breath came short and sharp as the delicious assault continued and it wasn't until silver spots flickered behind her eyes that she flipped the skirt over and panted, 'Need. Air.'

He extricated himself. 'I was just having fun,' he said with a wicked glint in his eye. 'Just like you.'

Laughing, she sat up. 'In the fairy tales, they never mentioned how the Princess got out of her gown for the Prince.'

'Going on history and the lack of underwear back then, I think the Prince just pulled up the skirts and helped himself while the Princess lay back and thought of England.' As his fingers found the tag of the dress's zipper, he kissed her gently. 'But I want to see and feel all of you.'

'So do I.' She reached for his belt and as her hand brushed his erection she suddenly flashed hot and cold. *Contraception.* 'You've got a condom, right?'

He paled. 'No.'

'What?' Panic and surprise took her voice up an octave. 'I thought you—'

'Never leave home without one?' He grimaced. 'Don't believe all the hospital gossip, Claire. This—' he flicked his long, dextrous fingers between them '—is an unexpected gift.'

His lack of a condom was in a way gratifying—he hadn't planned on having sex with anyone else—as well as devastating. They might not be having sex this evening after all.

'Mind you,' he said tightly as he strode to the bathroom. 'It might be a gift that doesn't get fully unwrapped.'

No. As she jerkily pulled open the bedside drawers on both sides of the bed, she heard him muttering, 'Bloody hell. There's enough shower gel here to wash an army.'

She reached into the second drawer expecting her fingers to touch a book but instead she felt a plastic case. 'Alistair.'

He stuck his head out of the bathroom, his

messy hair wild from the ministrations of her fingers. 'What?'

'Apparently, in the tradition of a hotel that's infamous for catering to the rich and famous, there's an aptly named "fun pack."' Laughing with delight, she waved it at him. 'Daniel wasn't wrong when he said we'd find everything we need. It's all here, plus breath mints.'

'Thank God for British ingenuity and organisation.' He walked back to the bed and the mood lighting cast tantalising shadows on his naked chest. 'Now,' he said with a sly grin, 'let's get you out of this dress.'

He made short work of the frock, freeing her in less time than it had taken her to pour herself into it and then he was gazing appreciatively at her new French lace bra and matching knickers. She sent up a vote of thanks to the sales assistant who'd encouraged her to buy them, despite the fact she'd spent far too much money.

'Don't think I don't appreciate lingerie, because I do,' he said, his eyes fixed on the demibra. 'It's just, right now I'd appreciate it more off you than on.'

With a proficiency she didn't want to examine too closely, he quickly divested her of her underwear. Attempting to match him, she unhooked his trousers and pushed his pants and underwear down to his ankles. He kicked them off and a thrill spun deep down inside her at the glorious sight of him before her—delineated pecs, washboard-flat abdomen, the tantalising trail of dark blond hair that arrowed down to the prize, which jutted out towards her, erect and ready.

I caused that, she thought in wonder, but before another thought could form, he'd killed the lights and was pulling her down onto the bed, rolling her into him in a tangle of limbs. His mouth honoured her, starting with her lips and then trailing along her jaw and down her neck before his tongue traced the hollow in her throat.

She shivered in delight, never having known such delicious sensations, and as much as she wanted to run her hands up and down his back and feel him too, she didn't want a moment's distraction from revelling in his touch. Besides, his mouth had closed around the aching and tingling flesh of her breast. An arrow of need darted deep, sharp and erotic, lifting her hips to his and bucking against him. Seeking him. Sliding her slick and ready self against him.

He groaned and raised his head. 'If you want me to go slowly, that's not the way to encourage it.'

'Fast, slow, I don't care.'

'God, Claire,' he ground out. 'I'm serious.'

'So am I.' Her heart hammered. 'Ever since that kiss I've—'

'Wanted this so badly I can't even think straight,' he said hoarsely.

'Yes.' She breathed out the word. 'Oh, yes.'

From the lights of the city that cast shadows in the room, she saw the agony of holding back glowing deep in his eyes. Her body thrummed so fast with need that her muscles quivered, desperate to close around him. She pulled her hands out of his grasp and picked up one of the distinctive blue squares. 'We've got more than one condom and we've got the night.'

'In that case, who am I to argue?'

She kissed him as she slid the condom along his silken length. Reminding herself this was her fantasy, and that he was hers to use for her pleasure, she rolled him over onto his back.

He rolled her straight back, capturing her hands again. 'I've fantasised for a long time about your legs wrapped high around me.'

She was awestruck. 'You have?'

'Do you have any idea what those shoes you wear do to me?' His voice was hoarse.

'I can put them on if you want?'

'Next time.' His voice was hoarse.

She gripped his waist with her legs, crossing her ankles above his back and he entered her tantalisingly slowly. Millimetre by millimetre, in and out, gently gaining depth until he filled her completely, she was almost screaming with frustrated pleasure. An unexpected sob left her lips.

He instantly tensed and concern pierced the fog of lust in his eyes. 'Are you okay?'

She tightened around him. 'I'm more than okay.'

It had been such a long time since she'd had sex. Since she'd experienced bliss quite like this. *It's never been like this.*

Her hips rose as she matched his rhythm, welcoming the length of him stroking her. She wanted to kiss him but sensation was taking over and her head thrashed from side to side as ecstasy built. The noise of their panting breaths fell away as the edges of her mind started to blur. Nothing existed except his touch and the addictive bliss that drove her on, promising euphoria. Her body spun ever upwards—twirling, rising, seeking and craving the ephemeral delight.

With a shout of wonder, she was lifted high out of herself, shattering into a thousand shards of silver that rained down all around her. As she fell back to earth, he jerked over her, crying out her name. As she raised her head to kiss him, she tasted salt and the joy of her own tears.

CHAPTER EIGHT

ALISTAIR COULDN'T STOP grinning but he knew he had to wrestle down the desire to beam from ear to ear before he arrived at the castle. If he didn't, his joie de vivre would invite nudges, winks and comments from all the usual suspects—like the porters who'd say, 'You're looking happier than you deserve to, guv.'

And he was happy. Ridiculously happy, but no one at the castle could know the reason for his good spirits. Especially not Robyn. As head of surgery, she'd have his guts for garters and the Royal College of Surgeons would be none too pleased either if they got a whiff of anything untoward. Not that either he or Claire considered what had happened between them to be anything other than marvellous.

After making love twice—the first time hot and explosive, the second time deliciously slow but oddly more intense—they'd fallen asleep. He'd woken to find her head on his chest and her hair strewn all over his body. Normally when he had sex with a woman, he tended to leave her bed soon afterwards, but with Claire's words— *one night*—clear in his mind, along with being in the neutral territory of the hotel, he'd fallen asleep and had slept surprisingly well.

He blew a few strands of her hair out of his mouth and nose, but his tickling breath must have woken her. She'd opened her sleep-filled eyes and a moment later—the exact second she'd remembered where she was—they'd dilated into pools of caramel sauce. It was as natural as breathing to stroke her hair. 'Good morning.'

She smiled, although it held hesitancy at the edges. 'Hi.' She raised her head so she could see the bedside clock and then gasped. 'No. Nine-fifteen? This is a little awkward.'

It should have been very awkward but for some reason it wasn't.

'Why?'

She sat up quickly, pulling the sheet with her. 'Oh, you know.' She gave an embarrassed laugh. 'With the dawn comes the unforgiving light.'

He laughed. 'You look deliciously sexy and sleep rumpled to me. I tell you what. We can always keep the curtains closed and pretend it's still the night.'

Two hot-pink spots appeared on her cheeks and she groaned. 'Is that a polite way of saying I have the remnants of last night's makeup halfway down my cheeks and wild and crazy bed hair?'

He thought she looked beautiful. 'Nothing that a shower won't repair,' he'd said, kissing her gently. 'Tell you what. Let's have a shower and some breakfast before we open the curtains and concede the night's over.' She stared at him for a long moment, her face giving away nothing. A stab of disappointment pierced him. 'Or not.'

She blinked a few times before making a sound that was half laugh and half discomfiture. 'Um... Al.'

All his life he'd been called Alistair and it was rare that anyone ever shortened it. If they did, he promptly corrected them, but there was something about Claire's accent, and the intimacy the contraction implied that kept him silent. 'Yes?'

'The dawn also brings reality. My disposable contacts are long gone and I don't have my glasses. Everything's out of focus. To be honest, I can't see much further than my fingertips.'

He laughed and pulled her in close. 'You don't have to see, Claire. Just feel.'

'Is that an invitation?'

'Could I deny a half-blind woman anything?'

She smiled the smile of a woman who'd just been given a box wrapped up in tissue paper and a bow, and she slid her hands up into his hair. Her fingers delved deep, firmly exploring his skull.

'Are you taking up phrenology?' he quipped.

Her fingers moved forward to his forehead. 'With this prominence, you'd be considered benevolent.'

'That's definitely me.'

She raised her brows as if disputing his claim, but the look in her eyes didn't match it. She continued her exploration, slowly tracing the orbit of his eyes before the stubble on his cheekbones slowed the progression of her fingertips. She traversed the length of his nose, drawing a little circle on the tip and then she outlined his lips and traced his jaw. As her fingers left a spot, she kissed it.

He relaxed into her light and gentle caresses and his mind slid away from all thought, sinking blissfully into the sensations and absorbing every single one of them. She moved her hands to the column of his neck and using both thumbs in a soft massage she swept outwards from the centre until she reached the base of his throat.

His now languid body pressed heavily into the mattress and his mind emptied, conscious of nothing except the pleasure of her touch. Her fingers were drawing delicious small and continuous 'e's along both of his clavicles, moving slowly but surely out towards his shoulders.

A shot of adrenaline pierced his languor and he thrust out his left hand, immediately capturing her right. He had no problem with Claire, the woman, touching him, but Claire, the doctor, was another matter entirely. He sure as hell had no desire to talk about what she was about to feel and instantly diagnose with her fingers. She'd ask questions—questions he didn't want to answer—and not only would it summarily end her delicious exploration of him, it would end their magical time together on a sour note. He had no intention of allowing that to happen.

Thank goodness she couldn't see very well. He pressed her hand to his mouth and kissed it before using his tongue to tickle her palm. She laughed and the musical sound surrounded him before sliding under his skin. As it trickled along his veins, he had the strangest sensation—something that made him feel different somehow—but with a beautiful and naked woman sitting astride him, he didn't pause to give it any thought.

Very slowly, he sucked one of her fingers into his mouth before releasing it and turning his attention to the next one. With each flick of his tongue, he felt her thighs tense and relax against his own and felt himself harden against her. As he released her pinkie finger he pressed her hand on his belly with her fingers splayed downwards.

She shivered and without hesitation she took the bait exactly as he'd hoped she would. Her attention was focused far from his shoulder and her fingers and mouth explored him until he begged for mercy. She rolled a condom on him and he rolled her under him.

Afterwards, they'd shared a tub and he'd cradled her back against him, keeping her hands firmly away from his chest. They'd blown bubbles of bath gel like little kids, delighting in the rainbow of colours as the bubbles floated above them. Food had followed and he'd consumed the largest breakfast he'd eaten in a very long time. He'd been unable to convince her that kippers were a treat.

'Bacon is a treat,' she'd said, savouring two poached eggs. 'Pancakes and maple syrup are a treat, but oily smoked fish? Not so much.'

'All that omega-3 is good for your joints and helps ward off Alzheimer's.'

'You forgot to mention reducing the risk of heart disease and stroke.'

He hadn't forgotten at all. His failure to mention the top two health risks had been deliberate. Not that omega-3 could have prevented his cardiac condition, but it could help stave off other complications.

'I prefer to get my daily dose of omega-3 from nuts.' With a theatrical shudder of her white-bathrobe-clad shoulders, she pushed the plate of kippers back towards him. 'Be my guest and eat mine.'

'Well, if you're forcing it on me…' He'd speared it with his fork before enjoying the fish on hearty seed-laden toast.

'Perhaps kippers are a bit like Vegemite,' she said reflectively.

'How so exactly?' he asked, wondering about the connection between the ghastly black stuff Australians loved and the cold-water fish.

'To enjoy either of them, perhaps you have to be raised on them from an early age.'

'You might be right,' he said with a grin. 'I ate kippers a lot growing up. They were Cook's favourite breakfast food.'

Her coffee cup stalled halfway to her luscious mouth. 'Cook?' She blinked. 'You grew up with a cook?' Her disbelief rode across her face and settled in her startled and out-of-focus gaze.

He regretted the slip of his tongue. What the hell had made him mention Cook? Trying to shrug away all the disparate emotions that always hit him when he thought about Englewood, he said with feigned easiness, 'We lived in the country.'

She laughed. 'And that's your explanation? In Australia, living in the country and having a cook are not automatically connected. Next you'll be telling me you had a nanny and you went to boarding school.'

'Guilty on both counts, I'm afraid.'

'And it keeps happening,' she said, sounding slightly bewildered.

'What keeps happening?'

'Me, feeling like I've stepped into the middle of an English novel from my childhood.' She slathered jam onto a croissant. 'I grew up in a town ringed by red dust. I'm the daughter of a mechanic and a secretary. My mother was an anglophile and she read me all the classics like *The Secret Garden*, *Wind in the Willows*, all the Roald Dahl stories and, of course, A. A. Milne. The idea of having a cook and a nanny was the stuff of stories, but you actually lived it. Tell me, did you have a secret garden?'

'There was a walled garden, but it wasn't very secret.' He gave a wry smile. 'My father used to tease my mother that she only married him for the garden. She certainly loved it and my earliest memories are playing hide-and-seek with her there.'

Claire's eyes lit up. 'Do your parents still live in the great house in the country?'

He tried to stave off the flinch but it came anyway. Not for the first time today, he gave thanks that Claire was extremely short-sighted without her glasses. 'No. Dad died when I was thirteen. Due to a complicated family will, we had to leave.'

'Oh.' Her hand shot out and rested over his. 'I'm sorry.'

'It was a long time ago,' he said, sliding his hand out from under hers and refilling their coffee cups.

She frowned. 'Thirteen's a tough age to lose your father.'

Yes. 'Fortunately, I had some excellent housemasters at school.'

She rubbed her temples and he swooped into action, needing to prevent her from asking anything else about his father. 'Headache?' he asked.

She nodded at him with a resigned smile. 'As wonderful as all of this has been, I need to get home to my glasses.'

'In that case…' He rose and pressed a button. The curtains smoothly opened to reveal a Sunday full of sunshine. They both squinted into the light.

'Oh, God,' Claire suddenly moaned. 'I have to go out into broad daylight in an evening gown.'

'No, you don't.' He pulled her to her feet and kissed her hair. 'I've bought us both a souvenir to remember our night.'

She grimaced. 'I'm not sure wearing the hotel bathrobe home is any less incriminating than the dress.'

'O ye of little faith,' he said, tucking some damp strands of her hair behind her ear. 'We're leaving wearing a set of monogrammed hotel gym gear.'

'They sell that?' She laughed. 'I love this hotel.'

He'd agreed with her.

That had been nineteen hours ago. The last words she'd said to him before she hopped into a cab were, 'See you at work, Mr North.'

'Morning, guv,' one of the porters greeted him as he entered the hospital.

'Morning, Amos.'

'Heard you had a good weekend.' The porter tapped his nose as if he was privy to some private information. Alistair tensed for moment but relaxed when Amos said, 'Saw your photo in the paper with that pretty nurse Ms Hobbes.'

'It was my job to dance with all of the nurses,' he said easily, telling the truth. 'And I went home alone.'

Disappointment flashed across the man's face. 'That's too bad, guv. Next time, eh?'

Alistair grinned and kept walking. When he arrived on Koala Ward, his team were waiting for him, including Claire. He knew she would have arrived half an hour ago to read the files.

She gave him the same quietly restrained smile she'd given him for the past two weeks—well, at work anyway. With her hair pulled neatly back in a ponytail, a fresh white coat and glasses perched on her nose she looked exactly the same as she'd always looked. Rising to her feet, she picked up her stethoscope and swung it around her neck. The bell came to rest on the V of her blouse and it snagged his gaze. Immediately, the memory of a sheer lace bra that left little to the imagination hit him so hard his blood swooped to his groin.

'Morning, Mitchell. Bailey.' His normal greeting sounded strained and he cleared his throat. 'I want an update on Ryan Walker.'

'He's not triggering the ventilator yet,' Claire said as a small frown made a V on the bridge of her nose. 'We're continuing with the treatment of sedation, ventilation and parenteral nutrition.'

'That's all we can do at the moment,' Alistair said. 'Right, Bailey, your turn.'

After the ward round finished and he'd spoken to the Walkers, he ducked into the nurses' tea room and grabbed a cheese and ham croissant. He needed the fuel before a busy morning in outpatients. He'd just brushed the last crumbs off his fingers when Dominic MacBride telephoned him.

'We need you and your registrar down here for a consult. Sooner rather than later if possible.'

'On my way.'

As he ran down the stairs, he was surprised to meet Claire on the third floor. 'On your way to A & E?'

She's hardly going to the circus.

She nodded. 'Yep.'

He opened his mouth to say, *I had a great time with you*, which was what he usually said to a woman he'd slept with and wanted to see again. He promptly swallowed the words, remembering he'd promised her what had happened wouldn't spill into their work world. Right now, they were clearly at work. He frantically sought for something else to say but pulled up blank.

What the hell was wrong with him? He was British, for heaven's sake. He'd been raised on polite small talk. It was a relief to arrive at the ground floor. He pushed open the heavy fire door for her. As she slipped past he breathed in deeply, drawing in her scent that reminded him so much of summer days on the Côte d'Azur. The tang of grapes, the softness of lavender and the refreshing fizz of lemon shot through him and he had to fist his right hand so as not to wrap it around her waist.

In the corridor, he fell into step next to her when Claire's brisk pace suddenly faltered. She abruptly stepped sideways as if she was avoiding something and bumped into him, knocking him off balance. He automatically gripped her hips to steady himself. As he did so, he noticed a man standing stock-still in the middle of the hallway staring straight at him and Claire.

It took him a moment to recognise who he was, but as his hands fell away from Claire, he realised it was Thomas Wolfe. He hadn't seen the paediatric cardiologist in years, so why the hell was he staring at them as if he'd just come face to face with his worst nightmare?

The painful intensity of Thomas's gaze gave Alistair pause, and without thinking he glanced over his shoulder. Rebecca Scott, the transplant surgeon, stood behind them, her face pale and tight.

'North. Mitchell.' She gave them a brisk nod of acknowledgment before striding past them. Without saying another word, she skirted around Thomas Wolfe and exited the corridor.

For a moment Thomas didn't move. Alistair was about to break the uncomfortable silence with a 'Good to see you again, Thomas,' when the man spun around, punched open the large plastic doors to A & E and disappeared.

'Wow. ' Claire's face was full of curiosity. 'Who was that?'

'Thomas Wolfe. He's a cardiologist. Worked here years ago. I got a memo this morning saying he's back. God knows why when the storm clouds of closure are hanging over the castle.'

'That's as may be,' Claire said thoughtfully. 'But something pretty big's going on between him and Rebecca. If looks were a loaded gun, one of us would be dead by now.'

'They used to be married.' He blew out a long sigh. 'Guess it must have been a messy divorce.'

'That's an understatement,' Claire said with a shiver. 'It's a perfect example of why people who work together shouldn't...'

Her cheeks pinked up, reminding him of how she'd looked two nights ago. More than anything he wanted to kiss her. 'Get married?' he said quickly, before she could say, *Have sex*. 'I absolutely agree with you, but surely that doesn't preclude enjoying each other away from the hospital.'

'I think we demonstrated that was possible.' Her clipped tone was at war with her expression.

'Then why are you sounding like it was a science experiment where we proved a hypothesis?'

She gave him a rueful smile. 'We agreed to one night.'

A spark of hope lit through him. 'We can always agree to one night again. Hell, we can agree to one night as many times as we wish.'

'Alistair,' she said sadly. 'That spontaneous woman on Saturday night wasn't the real me.'

He wouldn't accept that. 'I think that woman's always been very much a part of you.'

'You're just saying that so I agree to another night.'

'I'd love another night with you, but what I said isn't a line.' He really wanted to touch her but they were standing in a busy corridor and she deserved better than becoming the next topic on the hospital grapevine. 'I think that impetuous and risk-taking woman's been hampered by your dyslexia and buried by its secret.

'But it's not a secret any more, and more importantly, not everything in life can be planned.' He was intimate with the truth of that statement. 'Nor should it be because overplanning can deny you opportunities.'

He held his breath and waited for her to disagree or tell him to go to hell but she didn't say anything. Instead, she shoved her hands deep into the pockets of her white coat and rocked back on her fire-engine-red heels.

When she met his gaze again, the whirlpool in her eyes had stilled to a millpond. 'So, you're suggesting that outside of work I could benefit from some more practice at being spontaneous.'

He grinned, delight lighting through him. 'I'd be very happy to help you.'

'In that case,' she said with a tinkle in her voice, 'I'll be in touch.'

'When?' He tensed as the needy word left his lips. The moment was utterly foreign to him. He wasn't the one who ever asked a question like that—it was the domain of all the women he dated.

'When I'm feeling impulsive.' A momentary flash of lust mixed with promise in her beautiful eyes. And then it was gone and she was pushing her glasses up her nose and turning away from him saying, 'They're waiting for us in A & E.'

He watched her walk towards the plastic doors feeling slightly discombobulated. She'd just done to him what he'd done to so many women before her. He didn't like it one little bit.

CHAPTER NINE

CLAIRE SLIPPED OUT of bed and took a moment to watch a sleeping Alistair gently snoring. She smiled at him tucked up in pyjamas, finding it odd that he always wore them or a T-shirt in bed. She put it down to a British idiosyncrasy.

Padding out of the room, she pulled a throw rug around her shoulders, sat on the couch and reluctantly opened her computer. The recently unleashed woman who was living for the moment reprimanded her.

You have a man in your bed other women would fight you for. Why aren't you in there with him?

Because I've been having so much fun the last three weeks I'm behind with studying.

Pffp!

The pleasure-seeking woman pouted, sat down and crossed her arms as if she was taking part in a sit-in demonstration.

You've still got time.

Claire visualised the calendar and wasn't as convinced. Ever since she'd made that first booty call to Alistair on the Monday night after the ball, they'd met at least three nights a week. Sometimes she called him and sometimes he called her, but either way, they always seemed to end up in her flat rather than his. She was working on not letting that bother her, because this thing they shared was just sex. Did it really matter whose bed they tumbled into?

She'd gone into this affair with her eyes wide open. Her goal was to loosen the reins on her need to control everything in her life and to practise some spontaneity. And it was paying off—she'd definitely improved. Of course, she'd never be as laid-back as Alistair was at work but she was giving him a run for his money outside of it. They were having fun and enjoying each other and that's all it could be. Even if Alistair hadn't been the perennial bachelor everyone knew him to be, she wasn't easy to love.

Claire forced her attention to the podcast about endovascular coiling of an aneurysm, but as the professor's words droned on, her mind drifted. *Why is he a bachelor?* That thought had been popping into her mind more frequently of late, especially after days like yesterday. Alistair had texted her just as she'd finished handing over to Andrew at noon. She and her junior house officer were sharing a Saturday shift and she'd worked the morning. *If you're free, I've got a plan.*

As his plans so often occurred under the cover of darkness and involved them being horizontal, she'd been a bit stunned when he'd picked her up saying, 'I thought it was time you were a tourist.' He'd pointed the car towards the Thames and half an hour later she was standing in a pod on the London Eye. As the cantilevered observation wheel slowly rotated, she'd taken in the awe-inspiring view with her very own tour guide.

'This is amazing. I'm so excited I don't know where to look first.' Her back was snuggled into Alistair's chest and he had his arms wrapped firmly around her.

'Start with the easy and close stuff. There's Big Ben and the House of Commons.' He lifted his right hand and pointed. 'That big block of flats is Buckingham Palace and closer to the river is Horse Guards. That big column—'

'Nelson in Trafalgar Square.'

'Well done. Now cast your eye beyond the bridge and what can you see?'

'Our favourite hotel.' She smiled a secret smile and tilted her head back until he was looking down at her with a sexy gleam in his eyes. A delicious shiver roved through her, setting off tiny fires of desire. 'That was a great night.'

He kissed her and she started to turn into him

before she realised they were sharing this pod with strangers. 'It was one of my best nights,' he said throatily before reverting back into tour guide mode. 'Keep your eye on the river and you can see Tower Bridge and the Tower of London.'

She could see their familiar shapes but it was a modern building that caught her eye. 'What's that glass and black steel building?'

'The Gherkin. It's office space and apparently its design style is neo-futuristic.'

Claire laughed. 'Looks more like a rocket to me. I think I prefer the older buildings.'

It was a gloriously sunny day without a skerrick of the famous London fog. She could see for miles. 'Where were the Olympics held?'

'Stratford.' He pointed in the direction.

'And where did you grow up?'

He didn't instantly respond. It seemed to her that a tiny gap had just opened up between their bodies, interrupting what had been one continuous head-to-toe touch.

He eventually said, 'It's further than the eye can see.'

'Show me the general direction.'

The gap closed and his warmth was once again trickling through her without any little darts of cool air. 'My mother lives in Little Wilbraham.' As the pod dropped in height he pointed in the same general direction as Olympic Park. 'It's a tiny little village south-east of Cambridge.'

She remembered him telling her he and his mother had been required to move house when his father died. 'Has that been home since you were thirteen?'

'I've always considered it more Mother's house than mine.'

'Why?'

Did she remarry? Did you feel usurped? Did you clash with your stepfather?

She found herself hoping he'd reveal something so she could flesh out the vague sketch she'd drawn in her head of his childhood. Currently, he knew a lot more about the child she'd been than she knew of him.

'I suppose it's because I spent more time at school than I ever spent at Rose Cottage,' he said reflectively. 'We always spent part of the summer abroad, and once I'd finished school and went up to Oxford, it become a place I visited on short stays. Home's my flat in Notting Hill.'

The flat she'd never been invited to.

He suddenly spun her around in his arms and gazed down at her, his grey eyes dancing with anticipation. 'Are you ready for your next surprise?'

'There's more?'

'Of course there is. You deserve a London day out and it's my privilege to provide it.'

Her heart suddenly wobbled rather precariously in her chest. She kissed him quickly, forcing herself to concentrate on how warm his lips felt against her own rather than how very close she was to the edge of a cliff and a flashing orange danger zone sign.

Hand in hand, they'd exited the pod and walked back to the car, before re-crossing the Thames and making their way to Hyde Park. Alistair had produced a wicker basket complete with a rug, china plates and cups, champagne glasses, silver cutlery and cotton napkins. They'd picnicked in style by the Serpentine, sipping champagne, feasting on Scottish smoked salmon inside crusty buttered bread and peeled quail eggs and cheese. As they ate, they talked about the books they'd read, music they enjoyed, current political scandals and the many differences yet shared similarities between their two countries.

When Claire was almost certain she couldn't eat another thing, Alistair had delved back into the basket and with a 'Ta-dah!' produced two slices of chocolate and salted caramel layer cake and a Thermos of hot water to make tea. After they'd licked their fingers of every trace of chocolate and were utterly replete, they'd both fallen asleep in the treasured London sunshine.

Of all the times they'd spent together, yesterday afternoon had felt the most like a date. When

Alistair had suggested they head home, she'd almost said, 'To your flat?' What had stopped her?

She thought about it and she couldn't get past her gut feeling that the question would have caused awkward tension. She hadn't wanted to ruin what had been a perfectly lovely afternoon. When it came to talking about himself and his family, he seemed surrounded by a taut reserve that doubled as a permanent *Approach with Care* sign. So she hadn't pushed that they go to his flat. Instead, she'd agreed with him that heading home to Bayswater was a great idea.

In the glowing cerise and violet fingers of the setting sun that streamed through the window, they'd made love. *No, you had sex.* Sex was their thing—their selfish, living for the moment thing—when they lost themselves in pure pleasure and in each other. He always started by gently pulling her hair out of her hairband and removing her glasses and then he'd kiss her long and leisurely until every part of her quivered like a taut string under the ministrations of a bow. Each time they had sex, she determined yet again to keep her glasses on because Alistair didn't require soft focus in any shape or form. She ached to see all of his perfection in sharp relief, but the moment he kissed her, she lost all coherent thought, her glasses vanished and she found she didn't care at all.

As darkness had settled over the flat, declaring the day truly gone, and the lights had flickered on both inside and out, he'd pulled on his shirt and she'd prepared herself for his goodbye. Instead, he'd said, 'I make a mean omelette.'

'Do you?' she'd asked, tracing a line from his hand, along his forearm and up towards his shoulder.

'I do.' He captured her arm and pulled her to her feet. 'Come on. You can be my sous chef.'

He hadn't been exaggerating his skills—he did indeed make a fabulous omelette. After eating the savoury delight, they'd cuddled up on the couch—she with her head on his chest, he with his arm looped casually around her—and he'd made stealth moves on her popcorn. The entire afternoon and evening had been scarily normal. Anyone outside on the street who'd paused to peer in through the window would have thought they were a regular couple.

We are so not a couple. Couples share more than sex.

They shared stories, and although she'd told him about her dyslexia and growing up and he'd certainly mentioned that his father had died when he was young and he'd spent his adolescent years at boarding school, there was something in the way he'd revealed the information that told her it was just the tip of the iceberg. And yet he was a kind, generous and thoughtful man, so why was he still a bachelor?

And just like that, she was back to where she'd started and nowhere near close to knowing what made Alistair North tick. *There's a reason for that. And he doesn't want you to know it.*

This thing they shared was nothing more than a hedonistic fling. She knew she was just another woman in a long line with many before her and just as likely many more after.

It's fine. I'm using him to practise being spontaneous and impetuous.

Then why do you want to see his flat? Why do you want to know where the estate with the walled garden is? Where he spent his childhood? Why do you want to discover the date of his birthday and if he's a good son to his mother?

I don't want that. I only want his body.

A sound not dissimilar to hysterical laughter sounded faintly in her mind and she shoved the ear buds harder into her ears. She restarted the podcast and this time she listened intently to the lecturer as if he was the only voice in the world.

An hour later she felt a tap on her shoulder and she glanced up to see Alistair standing behind the couch, freshly showered and fully dressed. She pressed pause on the podcast as a sigh of disappointment rumbled through her. She'd have loved him to be padding around her flat wearing nothing more than a towel looped low on his hips so she could watch the play of bunching muscles dancing under his skin. But the man was always pulling a shirt on and covering up.

'Good morning.' With a sexy smile, he bent down and kissed her full on the mouth. 'You're up early for a Sunday.'

The shimmers and tingles from his kiss spun through her, making her feel far more alive and happy than she could remember. 'Exams are less than six months away.'

A slight frown pulled down his brows. 'I've been distracting you.'

She pressed her hand against his cheek. 'In the best possible way.'

He kissed her again but this time it was devoid of the usual intoxicating heat. Instead, it was infused with gentleness and something else she couldn't place. 'I'll leave you to get on with it.'

Despite knowing that she needed to spend the day studying, she was filled with a disproportionate sense of despondency. She was about to say, 'Thanks for yesterday,' when he said, 'I'll go and grab some fresh clothes and return with pastries and coffee from Tony's. Then I'll quiz you on…' He squinted down at her screen.

'Aneurysms.' Somehow, she managed to pluck the word out of her stunned mind.

He nodded, his face full of empathy. 'Tricky buggers, aneurysms.' Then he kissed her on the top of her head and said, 'Back soon,' before disappearing out the door.

As it clicked shut behind him, she stared at it, trying to make sense of what had just happened. Alistair had offered to help her study.

So? Nothing odd or unusual about that. He's a neurosurgeon.

But there was everything odd and unusual about it. Consultants didn't help their registrars study—that wasn't in the job description.

Neither was having sex.

The sex has nothing to do with work.

And it didn't. They'd both kept the two utterly separate. During work hours they didn't text or call each other and when they were alone they were too focused on enjoying each other to talk about work. But this offer to help her study came on the back of yesterday's generosity and thoughtfulness. It made her heart lurch dangerously close to the rickety safety rail balanced on the crumbling precipice.

If she wasn't careful, she was at very great risk of falling in love with Alistair North. Not only wasn't it part of the plan, it was exceedingly hazardous. Loving Alistair wasn't an option because she risked far more than just her job—she risked her heart.

As she recommenced the podcast yet again, the droning voice of the professor seemed to whisper, *It's too late.*

Alistair stood at the scrub sinks looking out through the glass and saw the broad back of Matthew McGrory bent over a trolley. As the plastic surgeon straightened and the porter wheeled the patient into the operating theatre, Alistair glimpsed the serious burn to the child's face.

Matthew then came barrelling through the double doors, his athletic build making short shrift of the plastic doors. 'Hello, Alistair,' he said in his gentle Irish brogue so at odds with his rugby player bulk.

'That burn looks nasty,' Alistair said as he lathered up his arms. 'How did it happen?'

'He's one of the Westbourne Primary School kids. Name's Simon Bennett.' Matthew flicked the taps on with his elbows. 'Poor bloody kid. It's tough enough that his parents' drug habit came ahead of him and that he's basically growing up in foster care, without the added burden of disfigurement by a facial burn.'

'You using spray-on skin?'

He nodded. 'Aye. It's phenomenal and that burn is much improved. Today I'm debriding an infection on his arm. It's best done in theatre. Rupert gives him a light GA and it minimises his pain.'

'The fallout of that fire's still haunting us,' Alistair said, thinking of Ryan.

'It is,' Matthew said quietly, 'but it also proved how much the castle's needed here in central London.' He rinsed off his arms. 'By the way, the fundraising committee owes you a debt of thanks. It was good of you to let Victoria sell off every part of your night to raise money.'

'No problem.'

'Did you at least meet someone you liked? Someone to have fun with?'

Alistair immediately thought of Claire and how much fun they'd had—were still having. He opened his mouth to give the usual quip—a standard shared between two men who have no desire to be tied down—but the words stuck in his throat. He put it down to his promise to Claire to keep their affair secret and out of the hospital.

'Mr North,' a nurse interrupted. 'Patient's under and we're ready when you are.'

'On my way,' he said, stepping back from the sink with both arms raised and a silent vote of thanks to the nurse.

'No rest for the wicked, eh?' Matt said, a friendly glint in his eyes.

None indeed.

Claire paced outside the lecture theatre, clutching her notes and the accompanying USB stick that held her presentation. As she walked, she concentrated on keeping the rolling nausea at bay. The day she'd dreaded had arrived and she was about to stand up in front of her peers and their consultants.

'I've arranged for us to present first,' Alistair had said to her two days ago at the end of a long operating list. 'After all, neurosurgery's the elite surgery and deserves top billing.' What he didn't say, but was clearly implied was, 'That way you get the presentation over and done with early and you can relax and enjoy the others.'

His discretion and kindness had just about undone her. He knew how much standing up in front of people terrified her and he'd done his best to try and minimise her trauma. It had taken everything she had not to throw her arms around him there and then in front of the theatre staff and shower him in kisses of gratitude. Instead, she'd said a brisk, 'Sounds like a plan,' from behind her surgical mask and hoped he saw her thanks clear in her eyes.

His eyes had twinkled as he'd said, 'Don't be late, Mitchell.'

The scrub nurse had laughed. 'Alistair, that's the pot calling the kettle black. You could take a leaf or ten out of Claire's book.'

Andrew Bailey, surrounded by a crowd of other junior house officers, walked past Claire and gave her the double thumbs up. He was clueless to the fact she was working very hard on keeping from throwing up the piece of toast and black tea she'd only half managed to finish at breakfast. Despite having committed the presentation to memory, she'd been up since five a.m., going over it *one more time* at least five times more.

She checked her watch. Where was Alistair? *Please don't be late today. Please.* The previously full corridor was now empty as everyone had entered the lecture theatre to take their seats. The toast hit the back of her throat and she gagged, forcing it back down.

What was wrong with her? This was even worse than the last time she'd had to present in Australia. Back there, no one had known about her dyslexia and she'd not only laboured under keeping it a secret, she hadn't received any support from her consultant. Today she was secure in the knowledge of Alistair's respect and understanding and yet she was desperately close to throwing up. It didn't make any sense. Then again, nerves rarely did.

Closing her eyes, she tried to focus on long, slow deep breaths so she could harness some desperately needed calm.

'Are you ready, Claire?' Alistair's voice sounded quietly behind her.

Her eyes flew open and she spun around as

frustration and relief tangoed fast in her veins. 'You're late!'

He checked his watch. 'I'm a minute early.'

'A minute isn't early,' she heard herself screech. 'It's barely on time.'

He raised his brows. 'Have you ever known me to be a minute early?'

Against the noise of her thundering heart booming in her ears and the agitation of her mind, she clearly heard, *No, not once.* He'd made a huge effort for her. Her heart lurched and she completely let go of the pretence that she liked him but didn't love him. It streamed away like the rush and gurgle of bath water racing down the drain. When Alistair made gestures like helping her study and arriving early, it was impossible not to feel her love for him fill up her heart and spill over into her soul.

Joy and heartache collided, crashing together in her chest. *I truly love him.*

'However, if you're going to stand here arguing the point with me, we will be late,' he said with envious ease, infuriating logic and absolutely no idea of her inner turmoil.

Her unwise love for him mixed in with her fear of public speaking, spinning her stomach like a tumble dryer. 'I think I'm going to throw up.'

'Nonsense, you're going to be fine,' he said with British exactitude. 'You're prepared. You know the work inside out, and if the worst happens, which it won't, I'm right there beside you.' He stretched out his arm towards the door and gave her a reassuring smile. 'Shall we go in and dazzle with them our findings?'

Claire didn't know if she was happy or sad that the symposium was over. Alistair, true to his word, had stood next to her but there'd been no need for him to step in—she hadn't faltered once. On Alistair's flippant but sound advice, she'd pictured the audience naked and it had helped. Whether it was that, her preparation, Alistair's presence or a combination of the three, it had carried her past her terror.

For the rest of the day, she'd floated on a sea of praise. Robyn Kelly, the head of surgery, had sought her out at lunch to congratulate her and strongly urged her to submit the paper for consideration at the international neurosurgery conference. Andrew had pumped her hand so enthusiastically that her shoulder still ached and she'd overheard Dominic MacBride telling Alistair that he wished his specialist registrar was as switched on as Claire.

Her boss had quipped, 'Of course she's brilliant. I taught her.' The man she loved had said quietly to her during the applause, 'Well done. We'll celebrate tonight.'

It was the first time he'd ever referenced their affair at work and rather than sending rafts of anxiety thudding through her, a warm glow of anticipation spread instead. When she stacked up all the little acts of caring he'd shown her over the past weeks, was his breech of their pact part of a growing affection for her? She hugged the thought tight as she closed her heart and mind to the warning. *He's known as the playboy surgeon for a reason.*

The afternoon sped by quickly with a full outpatients' clinic and now it was six in the evening. She'd called by Koala Ward to check for any outstanding IV orders and medication updates, and thankfully all was quiet. Her stomach rumbled, the noise reminding her that she'd not really eaten very much all day. This morning's nauseous nerves had killed her appetite and most of lunchtime had been spent fielding congratulations, leaving no time to eat. She'd munched on an apple during the dash to outpatients. It wasn't surprising she was now famished.

As she was rostered on until nine, she needed to stay close to the hospital but the thought of the cafeteria food suddenly made her feel queasy. Decision made, she grabbed her bag and said to Morag, 'I'm just popping over to the Frog and Peach to grab some dinner.'

'I'm glad you're accepting the house officers'

invitation.' The older woman gave her a motherly smile. 'There's more to life than work, Claire.'

'I'm a specialist registrar with exams looming,' she said with a wry smile. 'There is no life outside of work.' But as she spoke the words, she knew them to be a lie. Over the last few weeks, she'd most definitely had a life outside of the hospital. 'Page me if you need me.'

'I'm sure we'll cope without you for half an hour or so. I recommend the pulled pork nachos. They serve it with their famous pale ale barbecue sauce. It's delicious.'

'Thanks for the tip.' She didn't bother to mention that Andrew had invited her for a drink at the end of her shift, not dinner. Although she appreciated the offer, the moment she could get away for the night she was heading straight home.

Home to Alistair. As she crossed the road to the pub, she felt the grin of pleasure stretch across her face and her body leap in anticipation. He'd messaged her about a late supper featuring chocolate sauce. As much as she liked licking chocolate sauce from the top of ice cream and cake, she had a fervent desire to lick rich, dark chocolate sauce off Alistair.

Her cheeks immediately heated at the thought and she laughed. Six months ago, she could never have imagined herself being so sexually adventurous but practising being spontaneous was paying off in spades. *It's not that. It's Alistair.* And she knew it to be the truth. She'd had boyfriends before and there'd been the year with Michael, but no one had ever made her feel as accepted, safe and loved as Alistair. It meant she had no need to hold anything back and as a result she'd thrown herself heart and soul into this affair. She was utterly and deliciously in love.

Earlier in the day when she'd realised she loved him, gut wrenching worry had pulled at her, but not now. She'd gained an odd sort of peace in the knowledge that she loved him. Instead of trying to plan and control everything, instead of telling him how she felt or trying to find out if he felt the same way, she was just going to savour the feeling and the evening. After all, what did Alistair always say? Live every day as if it's your last.

The pub was a glorious historic building that had been in continuous operation since being built in 1823. Claire always laughed when she was told it was a young pub—it was still older than the oldest pubs at home. In typical English style it featured dark wooden panelling, ambient lighting, comfortable chesterfield couches and a dartboard. The noise from the Thursday night crowd came out to meet her as she stepped across the threshold and much of it was emanating from a spirited game of darts between the junior house officers and the hospital porters. Not surprisingly, the porters were winning.

She was depositing her dripping umbrella in the umbrella bin when a waitress walked past balancing four plates of delicious-looking food. She breathed in the aroma of meat, battered fish, chicken and cabbage and her stomach suddenly lurched, vanquishing her hunger. She gagged and her hand flew to her mouth. She gulped in air but the kitchen door opened again and this time the sight of the food had her turning and dashing into the ladies'.

A rotund woman in her forties glanced up from applying lipstick. 'You all right, love? You look a bit peaky.'

Claire didn't dare open her mouth until she was inside the cubicle. When she did, her stomach heaved its meagre contents up into the bowl. When there was nothing left to vomit, she flushed the toilet, closed the lid and then sat shakily on the closed seat, feeling sweat beading on her top lip and under her arms. The rest of her shivered.

A tap came on the door. 'You all right, love?'

Claire raised her head from her elbow-propped hands. 'I will be. Thanks for asking.'

'Was it sumfink you ate? The food 'ere's usually top-notch.'

'I've hardly eaten anything today,' she said, thinking about this morning as she opened the door of the stall. 'I woke up feeling nauseous but that was because I was nervous about work.' She flicked on the taps and splashed her face with water.

'I think it's probably more than just nerves, love. Either you've got a bug or a baby.' The woman laughed as she checked her hair in the mirror. 'Every time I was pregnant, the smell of fried food and cabbage always did me in.'

'I can't possibly be pregnant,' she said, thinking how she and Alistair had always used condoms.

The woman handed her some paper towels and her expression held a worldly air. 'Unless you've 'ad your tubes tied, love, or you're not getting any, there's always a chance of being up the duff. My old man 'ad the snip and nine months later I 'ad me third. At least you can find out fast these days. There's a pharmacy across the road.' With a final check in the mirror, she turned and walked back into the pub.

Claire stared at herself in the mirror. A pale face with dark rings under her eyes stared back. Surely she'd just picked up a bug? She worked with children and earlier in the week there'd been a minor outbreak of gastro on the ward. Even with best practice of hand washing, it only took one child to sneeze or cough on her to transfer the infection. That had to be the culprit of the nausea and vomiting. She couldn't possibly be pregnant—she'd had a period just a couple of weeks ago.

You had a light period.

I've been burning the candle at both ends.

A flutter of panic filled her and she forced it down. She was being ridiculous and letting an off-the-cuff comment by a stranger put the wind up her. Feeling sick and off-colour all day had a perfectly reasonable explanation. She was understandably tired because she hadn't slept well worrying about the presentation. This morning's nausea had been stress and she'd vomited just now because she was overhungry and exhausted. Or she'd picked up a virus. Either way, she was *not* pregnant.

However, the pharmacy the woman mentioned would sell jellybeans and electrolyte solution, both of which were good for gastro. She left the bathroom and retrieved her umbrella. Just as she stepped back out into the rain her phone buzzed with Koala Ward's number. Sam Riccardo was fitting. The jellybeans would have to wait.

CHAPTER TEN

CLAIRE LAY IN the dark bedroom snuggled up with Alistair in a languid fog of bliss. The champagne he'd bought sat unopened in the fridge next to the untouched celebration cake and the chocolate sauce. It wasn't that she didn't appreciate his efforts—she did, very much indeed. It was just that once she'd stepped into the flat, into his arms and he'd told her how amazing she'd been this morning before proceeding to nuzzle her neck and tell her the things he'd been wanting to do with her all day, they'd both lost interest in the food and the drink.

Her phone rang, bringing reality back into the room. With a groan, she rolled over to the bedside table and picked up the glowing device. 'It's the hospital.'

'I thought you were off-duty?' Alistair stroked her hair.

'I am.' She swiped the screen, silencing the ring tone. 'Claire Mitchell.'

'It's Andrew.' Her junior house officer's voice came down the line sounding decidedly shaky.

'You sound dreadful. What's up?'

'I've got a temperature and I've been throwing up for an hour. I need to go home but I'm on call tonight. I've rung three other people but two of them have the same bug and the other is covering for one of them. My patients are stable but can you cover if needed?'

Gastro. Andrew has gastro. She gave herself a virtual high five. 'Sure. Tell the ward and the switchboard and then go home.'

'Sorry, Claire.' He made a gagging sound. 'Got to go.'

He rang off abruptly, and although Claire knew she should be sympathetic, she started to laugh. It bubbled up on a wave of deliverance, and although she tried to stop it, that only seemed to intensify the feeling. Tears streamed down her cheeks, her belly tightened and her whole body shook as she was utterly consumed by amusement and abject relief.

Alistair gave her a bemused smile before rolling her under him. His warm grey eyes stared down at her. 'What's so funny?'

'Andrew's got gastro.'

He frowned at her, his expression confused. 'And that's funny how?'

She wiped her cheeks on the sheet and tried to curb her laughter. 'It's not funny for him.'

'But it is for you?'

She smiled up at him, eager to share the joke. 'I threw up tonight at the Frog and Peach and a random woman in the bathroom asked me if I was pregnant. Of course I knew the suggestion was ridiculous but just for a short time I was a little rattled. But Andrew has gastro and quite a few other castle staff have it too. So you can see why it's funny.'

She expected him to laugh with her and then tease her about being obsessive but instead his face tightened along with the rest of his body. He rolled away from her.

'I don't think the idea of you being pregnant is funny in any shape or form.'

She gave a wry smile. 'It was really more like a momentary possibility than an idea.'

'Jeez, Claire.' He suddenly grabbed his shirt, pulling it on jerkily before he reached out and switched on the lamp. 'That's semantics. You know that both scenarios would be a total disaster.'

Would it? A tiny part of her thought being pregnant might be the most wonderful thing to ever happen to her. Her practical side conceded that a pregnancy right now wouldn't be ideal but there was something in the aristocratic way he'd said 'disaster' that made her spine tingle.

'We're two adults having sex, Alistair. Contraception has been known to fail. Although we both know it's small, there's always an inherent risk.' She gave a light laugh. 'You're the one who's always saying not everything in life can be planned.'

He swung his feet to the floor. 'Children are the one exception.'

For someone who was impetuous, it seemed an odd thing to say. She sat up and pressed her hand gently against his back. 'But you're so great with kids. I'd like to think that if we'd had an accident and I was actually pregnant, we'd be a team.'

He lurched abruptly to his feet, moving away from her so quickly that her hand was left hanging in the air. 'A team? As in parents?' Incredulity dripped from the words, landing on her like scalding water and blistering her skin. He shook his head so hard that strands of his thick hair rose off his head. 'No. That is *never* going to happen.'

His emphatic words struck her with the biting sting of an open-handed slap and her heart cramped so tightly it was hard to breathe. Michael's words, which had faded to silence over the last few weeks, roared back loudly and in surround sound. *You're too hard to love, Claire.*

'I see,' she said grimly, feeling the sudden need

to cover up. Pulling on her pyjamas, she stood, pointing a shaking finger at him accusingly. 'So basically, I'm good enough for you to screw but I'm not good enough to be the mother of your children.'

He flinched and his face pulled into a grimace. 'I didn't say that. Don't put words in my mouth.'

'I'll just use the ones you inferred, then, shall I?'

'Claire.' His usually tender voice now spoke her name on a warning growl.

'Fine,' she said bitterly, hugging herself to try and stop the shaking. To try and silence the insidious voice of relationships past. 'Tell me exactly what it is that you're saying.'

He sighed, the sound patronisingly reasonable. It was the same sound people used when they believed they were dealing with a difficult person. 'Why are we arguing about a hypothetical situation? You're not even pregnant.'

Because you started it. The common childhood expression burst into her brain but the feelings behind it were anything but childish. 'Because if I was pregnant, we'd need to have this conversation.'

'This is crazy, Claire. It's all about *ifs* and *buts* and it's not worth our time.'

But suddenly it was very much worth her time

because she'd glimpsed something that scared her. 'What if I was pregnant?'

'You're not.' The words quivered with barely leashed restraint.

'No, but what if I was?' She scanned his face, trying to read it. 'What would you say?'

He suddenly looked wary. 'Would it matter?'

'Of course it would matter.'

He stared at her as if she was someone he didn't recognise. 'Are you telling me that if you were pregnant, you'd want to keep it?'

It. The pronoun battered her like a barrage of needles piercing her skin with sharp and biting stings. How could one tiny word emote so much? How could two innocuous letters combined draw such a precise line in the sand and place them clearly on opposite sides? To her, a pregnancy was a longed-for baby and the reactivation of a dream she'd believed to be covered in dust. To him, it was just an amorphous *it*.

'Of course I'd want to keep it.'

Horror and bewilderment streaked across his face. 'Why?'

She didn't have to think twice. 'Because it would be our child. Because I love you.'

He went deathly still and his handsome face lost its healthy colour, leaving behind a tinge of yellowy-green. 'You don't love me, Claire.'

The softly spoken words fell like the blow of

a hammer. They shattered any remaining delusional daydreams she may have been clinging to and they shattered her heart. 'I think what you meant to say was that *you* don't love me.'

He started pacing jerkily around the small room. 'This thing we've been sharing is fun, Claire. It's not love.'

She wasn't prepared to lie. 'For me it's been both.'

His hand tore through his hair and his face crumpled. 'Good God, Claire. No.'

She hated the crushing waves of despair that rolled in on her, bringing with them all the reminders that no matter what she did, or how hard she tried, it was never enough to be loved. Her breath came in short jerky pulls and she felt as if she was folding in on herself and collapsing down into a dark pit of hopelessness.

Her legs trembled like jelly to the point she reached out to the wall for support, but then her knees suddenly locked. Like a life preserver being thrown from a ship to a drowning person in a choppy sea, she saw and heard a collage of moments spent with Alistair.

You're a very good neurosurgeon.

It's your decision. If you have any doubts at all…

Don't believe all the hospital gossip, Claire. Are you okay?

I think that spontaneous woman's always been very much a part of you.

I'm right there beside you.

You deserve a London day out and it's my privilege to provide it.

It was one of my best nights.

Her mouth dried in shock. She may not have a vast experience of men, but she'd lived with Michael. During their year together all he'd done was find fault with her in so many ways and, oh, how he'd loved to tell her. She worked too much. She studied too much. Her friends were boring. She micromanaged their lives. She was inflexible. She stifled him with her need to control every minute detail. The list had gone on and on.

Right there and then she realised with the clarity of a fine-cut diamond that Michael had only considered their relationship in terms of himself. None of it had been about her, her feelings, her wants or her needs. Yet in a few short weeks, Alistair had considered her and cared for her in more ways than Michael had managed in a year.

Did Alistair love her but not recognise what he felt as love?

The thought snuck in and took hold, sending down a deep and anchoring root. If that was the case and she took her hurt and walked away now just to avoid the possibility of further pain, she might be abandoning an opportunity for happiness.

And if he doesn't love you?

Isn't it better to have tried and failed than to never have tried at all?

Yes. No. I'm scared.

It can't be worse than it is already. It might even be better. Fight for him. Open his eyes.

Tugging at the base of her pyjama top, she sucked in a deep breath. 'Actually, Alistair, the answer is yes. I do love you. I didn't intend to fall in love and the fact that I have lies squarely at your feet.'

'What?'

'You've only got yourself to blame.'

Bewilderment hovered over every part of his lean frame. 'What the hell are you talking about?'

She mustered an attempt at a smile. 'You've been so kind to me. You care.'

'Well, of course I bloody well care.' He agitatedly rubbed his stubble-covered jaw with his palm. 'I care for every woman that I date. That doesn't mean I've loved any of them. It doesn't mean that I love you.'

Her armour pinged with the hit but she pressed on. 'Will the world end if you admit that you love me?'

'Look, Claire,' he said in a voice she'd heard him use with junior staff at the hospital. 'You've got this all wrong. Somehow you've tangled up professional courtesy and mentoring with the fun we've been having. I can assure you, none of it is love.'

A distance she'd not seen before took up residence in his eyes. 'I'm not looking for love, Claire. I thought we were both very clear on that topic from the start. I've got a great career and a good life. I've got a flat in Notting Hill, a house in Provence and I can do what I want when I please.'

She pushed her glasses up her nose and stared him down. 'You forgot to mention the German sports car.'

'Exactly,' he said as if he thought she was being helpful. 'It's not designed for a baby seat. When you add up everything I have, why would I want to tie myself down by getting married and becoming a father?'

You're thirty-nine. Why wouldn't you want to?

'It's an impressive list of possessions,' she said, trying to sound calm, when in reality desperation was clawing at her. 'There's just one flaw with your argument. Your job, your houses and your car won't love you like a family.'

His eyes immediately darkened to the steely colour of storm clouds bursting with rain and tinged with the red of outback dust. 'Like your family loved you?'

The attack was swift and lethal but as the pain

seared her she somehow scrambled to tell the truth. 'My parents loved me, Alistair. They just didn't know how to help me.'

He grunted as if the explanation made no difference. Suddenly it was her turn to see everything through a red haze. 'I think that comment has far more to do with you than with me. Your father died when you were at a vulnerable age and your mother packed you off to boarding school. Is that love?'

'Don't you dare presume to think you know anything about me and my family.'

Anger radiated off him with the ferocity of a bushfire and she almost raised her hands to try and ward off the scorching heat. His reaction spoke volumes and she'd stake her life she was close to whatever it was that had him placing possessions ahead of people. 'The reason I don't know anything is because you won't tell me,' she said as calmly as she could. She reached for his arm. 'You helped me, Alistair. You listened and you didn't judge. Let me return the favour. Please let me help you.'

He spun away from her, breaking their touch. 'I don't need any help. Unlike you, there's nothing wrong with me.'

Visceral pain ripped into her, stealing her breath and spinning the room. The past tried to rise up and consume her but it stalled. Without a shadow of a doubt, the man who'd just hurt her so comprehensively wasn't the man she knew and loved. That man had always respected her. He'd given her opportunities and choices. Out of the work environment they were equals, so what the hell was going on now?

He's hurting.

But exactly what was hurting him and why, she had no idea at all. Whatever it was, it was old and gnarly with deeply tangled roots. It lived inside him, and the more she pushed to get close, the more it would lash out and slice her until all that was left of her was a bleeding mess of heartache and pain. She'd be the one left suffering.

Self-preservation knotted inside her. She'd worked too hard to allow him to destroy her fledging self-confidence and the irony of that thought wasn't lost on her. It had been Alistair's acceptance of her that had taught her to value herself. She jutted her chin. 'I never took you for a coward, Alistair.'

As he pulled on his trousers and slipped his feet into his shoes, his mouth tugged down at the edges, thinning into a hard line. It accentuated his cheekbones, making them blade-sharp in his face. 'I was perfectly fine before I met you, Claire. I'll be perfectly fine when I walk out this door.'

He quickly grabbed his wallet, phone and car fob before storming past her. 'Of all the women

I've ever fooled around with, I thought you were the one who truly understood because you put work ahead of everything. Us having sex was all about you learning to be spontaneous and having some hard-earned fun.' He laughed bitterly. 'And you were doing so well. I thought you were more like me after all.'

She jerked her chin high. 'You mean emotionally shutdown and hiding behind a collection of possessions?'

He threw her a filthy look, which she met head-on and batted straight back at him. 'Believe me,' she said cuttingly, 'I'm not that sad.'

Stalking to her front door he hauled it open. In the brief moment before he slammed it shut, the sound of tyres squelching on a wet road and the distant toot of a train drifted into the flat—the sounds of a perfectly normal London night. Only none of this came close to normal. This was the end of friendship, hopes and dreams.

The door closed with a thwack and a thick wave of silence rolled inside, enveloping her. Alistair was gone. He'd left her without so much as a backwards glance. He'd also left her love— abandoning it casually on the couch, on the bed and on every surface in the flat. It lingered in the air she breathed and the sense of loss overwhelmed her. She sank to the floor and let her tears flow.

* * *

'Morag!' Alistair roared through the closed door of the unit manager's office. His day was going to hell in a hand basket and it wasn't even ten o'clock in the morning.

Things went to hell last night.

But he wasn't spending any more time thinking about how things between him and Claire had gone pear-shaped so quickly and so unexpectedly. He'd spent the dark wee hours consumed by it, trying to work out how he'd missed the telltale signs. Good God, he had a thesis in detecting signs from women wanting marriage and babies but he had missed the clues. Claire was just like all women and she wanted what he couldn't give her. 'Morag!'

Her dark-haired head appeared around the door thirty seconds later. 'Did it slip your mind that you can walk the twelve steps from here to the nurses' station if you wish to speak with me?'

'Humph,' he grunted as he opened a filing cabinet drawer. 'I'm going to France.'

Surprise crossed her face. 'When?'

An hour ago. 'Tonight if I can get a booking on the Eurostar. Where the hell are the leave forms?'

Morag walked calmly into the office, smoothed her uniform and sat down. 'Alistair, didn't you read the memo from the board?'

He riffled through the neatly labelled manila

folders. 'Which one? They've been coming in thick and fast ever since the proposed merger with Riverside.'

'The one where they cancelled all leave requests because we've barely got enough staff to keep operating as it is.'

He didn't care about any of that. He had to get out of the castle and he had to get out now. He needed the space and serenity that Provence always offered him. He needed to find his equilibrium. He desperately needed to find the solid foundations he'd rebuilt his life on after almost losing it five years ago. 'Surely that doesn't include consultants.'

She gave him a pitying smile. 'I know it's a rarefied atmosphere up there at the top of the tree, but this time you have to slum it down here with the rest of us. The board isn't paying for annual leave and nor is it paying for covering staff. France will have to wait until your next three-day weekend.'

I can do what I want when I please. His haughty statement from last night came back to bite him. *You know your job never allows you to take off at a minute's notice. Your weekends in France are blocked out at the start of each year.*

He closed his eyes to the spotlight on the fact he did plan some things. 'If the board's not spending any money, then what about this rumour that Robyn's flying in some hotshot Italian paediatrician?'

'The duke?' Morag grinned. 'Apparently they've been good friends since medical school. He's coming as a PR favour to Robyn and using his own coin.'

He sighed, seeing his out closing fast.

'Besides,' Morag continued, 'even if the board was approving leave you couldn't go today. Both Bailey and Mitchell are down with gastro along with three of my nurses.'

Claire's not in. He hated the relief that he didn't have to face her today. Hell, he shouldn't need to feel relief. She'd been the one to move the goalposts on him and change every single rule of their game. If she hadn't done that, if she hadn't pushed him about babies and about his family, then he wouldn't have needed to speak. He wouldn't have said the unforgivably cruel thing to her that fear had driven out of him.

Hell, he could still see her beautiful but tortured face every time he closed his eyes. It made him sick to his stomach. He wanted to apologise to her but if he did she'd expect an explanation from him as to why he'd said what he said. That would immediately take them back to square one, more arguing and even more distress. He'd survive but he wasn't sure she would. He didn't want to risk it. He couldn't bear to hurt her all over again.

No, it was better to say nothing and make last night the clean break. She'd nurse her pain into a fulminating rage towards him, which would grow into hatred and loathing. The result would be abhorrence, which would keep her far, far away from him. He expected her letter of resignation to arrive in his in-box by the end of the working day. All in all, it was the best possible outcome for both of them. With his condition and his family history, he couldn't offer her marriage and babies and she deserved to be free to find someone who could.

His mind threw up a picture of a faceless man and a flash of bright green light burst behind his eyes. He squeezed them shut against blinding pain and automatically rubbed his temples with his forefingers.

'Is there anything I can help with, Alistair?' Morag asked, her usually taciturn tone softening.

A new heart. 'No. There's nothing for it but to get out there and be junior house officer, registrar and consultant all rolled into one.'

'Be extra meticulous with hand washing,' Morag said, following him onto the ward. 'We don't need anyone else getting this bug.'

CHAPTER ELEVEN

CLAIRE MUNCHED ON dry biscuits and reread a list she'd started at three a.m. when she hadn't been able to sleep. That had been twelve hours ago and no matter which way she came at it, she couldn't get the list to clearly state what she willed it to. What she wanted more than anything was to jump online and book a flight back home to Australia. She wanted to put seventeen thousand kilometres between her and Alistair and the constant reminder that he didn't love her. She tried to find some reassurance in the fact he didn't love someone else either, but that only made her feel desperately sad for him. For some reason he seemed hell-bent on not allowing himself to love anyone.

The thought of spending another three months working side by side with him most days made it hard to breathe but the thought of giving up her scholarship and returning home a failure was worse. She'd fought so hard for the scholarship and the prestige that went with it, and besides, she still had things to learn. Trying to explain to her family why she'd given up London when she'd talked excitedly about it for months would take more energy than she could muster. Trying to talk her way around the fact she'd left the tutelage of Mr Alistair North at job interviews back in Australia would be equally hard. The panel would give her uneasy looks and ask the hard question, 'Why, when you were so close to qualifying, did you throw this opportunity away?'

When she heard the truth embedded in the words—*I'm putting a broken heart ahead of my career*—she knew what she had to do. Right now, in the detritus of her personal life, her career was the only thing she had left to hold on to and guide her. The scholarship lasted ninety more days, less if she subtracted her rostered days off. She sipped her lemon and ginger tea and sat a little straighter. She could do this. She would do this. In fact, she'd start as soon as she stopped throwing up.

Actually, she hadn't thrown up since last night, and although she'd felt a little nauseous this morning, it had passed by ten and she'd wolfed down a big breakfast. She'd be back at work bright and early in the morning but meanwhile she'd check her roster and count the actual number of days she had left at the castle. Opening her calendar on her computer she looked at the whole year displayed in four neat columns. Blue denoted today, green was days off, yellow was payday, purple was when her rent was due each month, brown was the fast approaching date of her exams and red was her period.

All of it made for a heartening and colourful display that was balm to an organised person's soul. Just glancing at the planner made her feel secure and slightly more in control. Who needed spontaneity? There was no pattern to it, which by its nature was not at all reassuring. Cross-referencing with her roster, she clicked her mouse and added in her days off for the next six weeks.

Job done, she sat back and enjoyed seeing the patterns all the different dots created. She suddenly lurched forward closer to the screen and adjusted her glasses, blinking at a red dot. Her period had been due on the tenth. She knew for a fact it hadn't come on that date. It had come earlier but she'd been too busy being spontaneous to realise quite how early it had come.

And it was very light.

Her stomach rolled. *Implantation bleed.* The thought she'd dismissed so easily yesterday was a lot harder to shift today. Was what she thought was a light dose of gastro not gastro at all? Was she pregnant? Was what would constitute Alistair's disaster and her not unwelcome surprise a reality?

Or not. It wasn't like her period was always

clockwork regular. There'd been times when it was a bit hit and miss, and after all, she'd moved continents and was working long hours in a stressful job. Plus, they'd always used condoms and to her knowledge no condom had broken.

There was that one time you straddled him before the condom was on.

She bit her lip. Was that all it took?

Her contraceptive lectures reverberated in her mind. *Oh, yes, it actually took less.* She tasted blood. If she was pregnant, Alistair had made it very clear to her that he didn't want to have a child with her.

It's not you, she promptly reminded herself, determined not to let past beliefs pull her down. She knew that all the way to her soul. Alistair didn't want to have a child with anyone. *So why does he work with kids?* So often, people who didn't want children were uncomfortable around them and avoided them as much as possible. Alistair not only worked with them, he was relaxed around them and he had the special skill of being able to calm a sick and terrified child. He'd ace fatherhood so why didn't he want children?

No answer was obvious and none made any sense. She couldn't help but wonder if all of it was connected to losing his father. She was intimately acquainted with childhood beliefs getting tangled up in adult lives and skewing them. Alistair had helped her see that in her own situation but he wasn't allowing her to help him. He refused to let anyone get close enough to offer any insight.

She was under no illusions. The reality was that if she were pregnant, she'd be embarking on the difficult but rewarding path of a single, working mother.

And if you're not pregnant?

I'll be relieved.

An empty feeling ringed with sadness tumbled through her, leaving an ache everywhere it touched. She gave herself a shake. Of course she'd be relieved if she wasn't pregnant. She had to be, didn't she?

'Argh!' The sound reverberated around the flat. There were too many *what-ifs* on both sides of the argument. There was only one definitive way to end this constant circular process and find out for certain if she was pregnant or not. Grabbing her phone, her keys and her handbag, she dashed out of the flat.

Yesterday, Alistair had welcomed the extra workload generated by Bailey and Cla—Mitchell's absence as it meant he hadn't had to think about anything other than work. Not that he needed to think about anything other than work right now, he reminded himself crossly, swiping the air savagely as he played solo virtual tennis in the quiet Koala Ward's lounge.

He'd spent the evening playing with the kids but they were all tucked up in bed now having been hustled away by the night nurse who liked the order of routine. He should have gone home then but the thought of an empty flat had kept him in the lounge playing game after game. He was determined to beat the machine. Determined to get thoughts of Claire out of his head.

Damn it, she wasn't the first woman he'd broken up with. She wouldn't be the last.

Other breakups didn't touch you. This one has.

He refused to acknowledge that. Hell, he'd dated other women for longer than he'd dated Claire so he had no reason to be affected by this breakup. The two of them wanted different things out of life. She had a choice in wanting a family, but he did not. End of story. Move on. Find someone else to have fun with. It wasn't like there weren't plenty of candidates to fill Claire's place.

Just this morning, he'd been called down to do a consult in the cardiothoracic ward, and while he was trying to locate the child in question, he'd come across Maddie, the pretty and chatty physiotherapist he'd sat next to at the ball. She was working with Penelope, the cute little girl with the sunny disposition who'd been in and out of hospital all her life. She'd become one of the cute-as-a-button, tug-at-the-heartstrings faces of sick children in the *Save Paddington's* campaign. Her photo, along with others, was on posters and billboards all around town.

Penelope, who was wearing a pink tutu, lay with her head and chest tilted downwards while Maddie's cupped hands postured and percussed her patient's chest, loosening mucous and easing the child's breathing.

'Hello,' Penelope said with a big smile. 'You're not one of my doctors.'

He smiled at her precociousness. 'I'm Alistair. I'm a brain doctor.'

The child considered this. 'My brain works really well. It's my heart and lungs that don't work so good.'

'Hello, Alistair,' Maddie had said with a wide smile as if she was protecting him from a difficult reply. 'Where have you been hiding lately? I haven't seen you since you stole my bread roll at the ball.'

'Oh, I've been busy,' he said, feeling oddly self-conscious. Part of him wanted to say, *With Claire*. 'You know how it is.'

'I do.' She smiled again and this time her chocolate eyelashes fluttered at him. 'But all work and no play makes for a very boring life. I'm a big fan of breaking up the work with a bit of fun. I've heard you're of a similar mind?'

You bet I'm having fun. Claire's throaty voice filled his head and he found himself comparing Maddie's flirting green eyes with Claire's studious yet sexy caramel ones. The physiotherapist's came up lacking. 'I better go and find Olivia McDermott,' he'd said, backing quickly out of the room.

A few short weeks ago he'd probably have taken Maddie up on her offer. *Before Claire.* Feeling warm, he loosened his tie and took another swipe at the virtual ball, thrusting his arm out hard and fast. Now, it was officially *After Claire*, except the damn woman was still at the hospital. All day yesterday he'd waited for her resignation to ping into his in-box, planning to expedite her leaving as quickly as possible. It hadn't arrived. The first thing he'd done when he'd hauled himself out of another fitful night's sleep this morning was to check for the email. It still hadn't come.

Despite that, he'd been stunned an hour later when he saw her standing next to Bailey, waiting for him on the ward. Her oval face had been slightly paler than usual but determination had squared her shoulders, rolling down her spine and spearing through her gorgeous—ridiculous— high heels to plant her firmly in place. All of it had said, *I'm not going anywhere.* It had rendered him momentarily speechless.

He hated that she'd said, 'Good morning, Alistair,' before he'd been able to give his usual nod and greeting. From that moment, he'd felt as if he was on the back foot for the rest of the round and that she'd been directing the play. Hell, even Bailey, who looked like death warmed up, had been less distracted than him.

At the end of the round when everyone had scattered he'd found himself asking her quietly, 'Are you sure you're well enough to be back at work?'

'Absolutely,' she'd said with a return of the crispness that had been such a part of her when she'd first arrived from Australia. Then she'd looked him straight in the eye and added, 'I plan to make the most of my remaining seventy-two working days here at the castle.'

His mouth had dried at her announcement that she wasn't leaving. She was going to be at work five days a week for the next three months and he couldn't do a damn thing about it. But he knew women and a jet of anxiety streamed through him. 'You do know that your staying makes no difference to us?'

Her eye roll was so swift and strong that the floor felt like it had moved under his feet. 'No need to worry, Alistair. You made your feelings abundantly clear. Besides, I learned from the master on how to clearly separate work and play without any inconvenient overlaps. I'm here because it's the best place for me to learn. Everything else is immaterial.'

And he *was* the master, so why in heaven's name did his mind keep slipping back to the fundraising ball and the subsequent nights they'd shared. *Because it was good sex.*

This time his subconscious gave an eye roll.

If it was just about the sex, why do you treasure the laughter and time shared on the picnic by the Serpentine? Why did you watch a chick-flick with her on the couch? Why did you spend whole nights at her flat? You've never done that with a woman before.

Anger stirred and he swiped the air again with an even harder thwack, sending the virtual ball scudding back across the screen. It suddenly looked out of focus and he blinked to clear his fuzzy vision. Was it rather warm in here? He threw off his tie without missing a point.

Remembering fun times with Claire didn't mean anything more than that he liked her and enjoyed spending time with her. When had that become a crime?

And what do you fondly remember doing with McKenzie, Islay, Rebecca, Eloise and Leila? Shall I go on?

Shut up.

He served with gusto, slicing through the air

so hard his arm hurt. Sweat beaded on his brow. He leaped around the lounge, volleying the virtual ball, determined to beat the damn machine.

Will the world end if you admit that you love me?

Claire's distinctive voice with its rising inflection was so loud in his head she may as well have been in the room with him. *Yes, damn it. It will.* He couldn't love her because if he did, then his carefully constructed new world—his post-ironman world—would tumble in on itself and bring with it all of the old pain. Pain he'd already endured once before. Pain he didn't intend to deal with again and he sure as hell wouldn't inflict it on anyone he loved.

And you love her.

The reality hit him so hard he felt light-headed and the room spun. The game buzzed at him, telling him he'd missed a shot. He started over, serving fast and faulting. He blinked away double vision, suddenly feeling unbelievably tired and cloaked with an overwhelming sense of fatalism. What did it matter if he loved Claire? Nothing good could come of it so there was no point telling her. He'd survived worse and he'd survive this. In seventy-two days she'd be gone.

'Alistair?'

Heat and cold raced through him at her voice but he didn't turn. Instead, he kept playing despite feeling that with each shot it was increasingly difficult to raise his arm. 'Claire?'

'Is it possible to add Harrison Raines to tomorrow's surgical list?'

'Fine.' He took another swipe with the plastic racquet and the room listed sideways. He staggered, fighting to stay upright.

'Are you okay?'

'Fine.' But the word echoed in his head. He didn't feel fine at all. The edges of his mind filled with grey fog. The racquet fell from his hand and he reached for the back of the couch to stop himself from falling.

Terror gripped him. Memories assaulted him. It had been a long time but he knew this feeling. He tilted sideways.

'Alistair!' Claire yelled his name as he fell.

After that everything was a blur as he slipped in and out of consciousness. He heard the thud of shoes on linoleum. Felt Claire's hand on his throat, seeking his pulse. Heard her say, 'God, his pulse is twenty-eight.' He recognised Bailey's voice yelling to get the crash cart.

'Alistair.' Hands shook him. 'Al. Do you have pain?'

Claire's beautiful face floated above him and he tried hard to fix it so it was still. He couldn't manage it.

Was this it? Had his borrowed time come to an

end? *No!* He didn't want to die, but he already felt disconnected from his body as if he was on the outside and looking down on everyone frantically trying to save him. With a monumental effort he tried again to bring Claire's beautiful face into focus. Behind her sexy thinking-woman's glasses, her eyes burned with terror and pain. He wanted to change that.

It was suddenly vital to him that his last word to her wasn't a terse, 'Fine.' He didn't want her to remember their last real conversation when he'd cruelly said, 'Unlike you, there's nothing wrong with me.' Oh, the irony.

'Claire.' His voice sounded far, far away but she must have heard him because she lowered her head to his.

'It's okay, Al,' she said frantically. 'I refuse to let anything happen to you. You're going to be okay.'

He wanted to lift his hand to her cheek and feel her soft skin against his but he lacked the strength. 'I… Love… You.'

The last thing he heard before his hearing faded was her choking cry and then everything went black.

CHAPTER TWELVE

As Claire stared at the contents of the St John's Hospital vending machine, she knew down to the tips of her toes that she never wanted to relive the last few hours ever again. *Not quite.* She smiled as she dropped coins into the machine. She'd happily relive hearing Alistair say quietly but clearly, 'I love you.' Was there anything more truthful than words spoken by a man who thought he was dying? She didn't think so. He loved her and she'd been right about that; however, it brought cold comfort when she'd been desperately worried she might never have the opportunity to hear him say them again.

Selecting orange juice, cheese and biscuits, and chocolate, she sent up another vote of thanks that by a stroke of luck or, as Thomas Wolfe had said to her, due to 'the mountain of unrelenting paperwork' that he'd still been at the castle at ten-thirty last night. Not only had he accompanied Alistair in the ambulance, he'd been very generous to her. As she wasn't family, without his consideration she'd have been denied any information about Alistair's condition and certainly not been allowed in to see him. Not that she'd seen him yet, but she lived in hope. Meanwhile, Thomas had reassured her that the surgery had gone well.

Along with Alistair's collapse had come a lot of answers to unasked questions. Why he was so hell-bent on living for the moment, although it seemed an excessive response to his condition. Then again, who was she to judge?

She unwrapped the thick and gooey chocolate-coated caramel bar and just as she bit into it a nurse walked over and enquired, 'Dr Mitchell?'

'Thaff's me,' she stuttered, using all her facial muscles to haul her teeth out of the caramel.

The nurse caught sight of her food stash and shot her a sympathetic smile. 'You got the five a.m. sugar drop? I get it too. Always feel a little bit nauseous at this time of the day.'

Claire nodded, still battling the quicksand-like properties of the caramel.

'Mr North's just waking up now,' the nurse continued. 'As his mother isn't due to arrive until midmorning, Dr Wolfe said you could sit with him.'

Bless you, Thomas. 'Thank you.'

They walked the length of the ward from the waiting area to the nurses' station and the nurse pointed to the door opposite. 'He's in there. I'll be in shortly to do his observations.'

Claire opened the door and stopped abruptly just inside. Alistair, always so vital and full of life, lay semi-upright in the narrow hospital bed. A sheet was pulled up tightly to his waist and a white hospital gown took over from there covering his torso to his Adam's apple. His face held slightly more colour than the cotton but not by much. Wires connecting him to the monitor snaked out from under the gown along with the IV that was connected to a pump that buzzed and purred. The rhythmic beep of the monitor, representing each life-giving heartbeat, broke the silence of the room.

Although she'd seen similar scenarios over and over since her first hospital visit as a medical student all those years ago, this was the first time someone she loved lay connected to all the high-tech machinery. Her heart beat faster in her chest and it took every gram of self-control she had not to rush over and throw herself at him and say, 'You scared me so much.'

Besides the very unwise idea of body slamming anyone who'd just undergone surgery, she knew that words like *You scared me* and *Never do that to me again* were not going to work in her favour. Alistair loved her but that hadn't stopped him walking away from her once before. She wasn't giving him a single excuse to do it a second time.

Walking slowly, she sat herself in the chair by the bed and slid her hand into his. He stirred, his head turning, and his eyes fluttered open. 'Welcome back.' She smiled, squeezed his hand and added softly, 'I believe you love me.'

Alistair's mind fought the pea-soup fog that encased it as he watched Claire's mouth move. Then her words hit him and everything rushed back. The virtual tennis. His dizziness. His almost certain belief that he was dying.

I love you.

His hand immediately moved to his left shoulder, his fingers frantically feeling for the small box-like device that had been part of him for the last five years. The shape and scar he'd hidden from Claire. All he could feel was adhesive tape and discomfort.

'It's gone,' Claire said matter-of-factly. 'Thomas removed it.'

He didn't understand. If Thomas had removed his pacemaker he'd be dead. But he couldn't be dead because he could feel the warmth of Claire's hand and the softness of her skin against his. 'If it's gone, what's keeping me alive?'

'The world's smallest pacemaker. It's wireless,

and it's sitting snugly in your right ventricle doing its job perfectly.'

'Wireless?' He knew he sounded inane but he was struggling to piece everything together.

She nodded and squeezed his hand again. 'Tell me. Exactly how long had you been playing virtual tennis when I arrived to find you on the verge of collapse?'

He thought back and automatically scratched his head, noticing the IV taped to the back of his hand. 'I'm not sure. Some of the kids wanted a tournament so I organised it and I played too. We started before dinner and kept going until Sister Kaur hustled them off to bed. I suppose I stayed a little bit longer after that.'

She made a sound that was half a groan and half despairing laugh. 'Alistair, that adds up to about five hours.'

He shrugged and the stitches in his shoulder immediately pulled. *Ouch.* 'So? I had the time. It's just swiping a plastic bat through the air. It's not like I was lifting weights for hours on end.'

She dropped her head for a moment before lifting it and pushing her glasses up her nose. She gazed at him, her eyes full of love and affection with a hint of frustration. 'I know it wasn't weightlifting or rugby but substantial repetitive action for that length of time isn't recommended for people with pacemakers.'

The events of the evening came back to him and he started joining the dots. 'I should have gone home but I was procrastinating. I didn't realise how long I'd been trying to beat that bloody machine.' *I was too busy thinking about you.* 'Did I damage a lead?'

'Thomas will explain it all to you but he thinks it's more likely you exacerbated a fault. The good news is your new pacemaker's titanium. There are no leads and the battery and pulse generator are all combined into one tiny device the size of a pill.'

He glanced at the monitor and saw the perfect run of sinus rhythm. 'It's working.'

'It's working very well indeed.' She winked at him. 'So now. Back to the fact that you love me.'

The relief at being alive took a hit from reality. God, how was he going to get out of this situation without hurting her? Without hurting himself. 'I thought I was dying.'

She didn't flinch and she didn't break her gaze. 'I know.'

A long sigh shuddered out of him. 'Now that you know all about my secret time bomb, you can understand why me loving you doesn't change a thing.'

She pursed her lips. 'I disagree. I think it changes everything.'

He threw his arm out towards the monitor and

the pump. 'You saw me collapse. You worked on me. You know I could die at any moment and I refuse to put you through that.'

'So, what? We just live miserable lives apart and when I die before you at ninety, then you'll realise what a dumb idea this is?'

He pulled his hand away from hers, needing to break the addictive warmth that promised what he couldn't have. 'I'm not going to live until ninety.'

'You don't know that.'

But he did. 'Claire.' He sighed again. 'You deserve a long and happy life with someone who can give you healthy children. Someone who will be around to see them grow up. I can't promise you either of those things.'

Her mouth pursed. 'The pacemaker overrides your SA node's propensity not to fire. With that sorted and without pesky leads getting in the way of your—' she made quotation marks with her fingers '—"live for the moment" obsession of playing virtual tennis for five hours, then the odds are in your favour to live a long life.'

He dropped his gaze, wishing it were that simple.

Suddenly two deep lines carved into her intelligent brow. 'It's not just the pacemaker, is it?'

Every other time she'd pressed him for information he'd been able to deflect or walk away. Today was different. He wasn't just physically trapped in a hospital bed hooked up to equipment; he was also trapped by his declaration of love.

'This is something to do with your father, isn't it?'

His heart raced. 'Why did I fall in love with a MENSA member,' he muttered darkly.

She gave a wry smile and raised his hand to her lips. 'Because I'm good for you and you're good for me.'

And he recognised the truth in her words but it wasn't enough to convince him that he should drag her down with him. 'Dad dropped dead at forty-seven from a myocardial infarction.'

'That's young.'

'Exactly. It dramatically changed my life and my mother's. We didn't just lose Dad, we lost our home and everything familiar. My grief-stricken mother retreated into herself and it took her a long time to tread a new path without him. She did the best she was capable of doing but I ended up fatherless and half motherless for many years. I wouldn't inflict that on any child.'

He'd expected her to offer soothing murmurs but instead she asked perfunctorily, 'Did he have an arrhythmia like you?'

'Not that we knew, but given he just dropped dead with no warning, it's safe to assume that he did.'

She frowned. 'So, no episodes of dizziness? No pacemaker?'

'No,' he said irritably. 'I thought I'd established that. He was fit and healthy and then he was dead.'

She ignored his terse tone. 'How old was his father when he died?'

'Seventy-five.'

'Heart attack?'

'No. Tractor accident.'

'Alistair, have you ever read your father's autopsy report?'

He was getting sick of the interrogation. 'Of course not. I was a child.'

'Exactly,' she said emphatically, her eyes suddenly shining. 'You were a kid.'

'You're not making any sense.'

'Okay.' She tucked some hair behind her ears. 'Do you remember when I was telling you about my fabulous mentor, Strez, and how he freed me from Gundiwindi's preconceived ideas? You said, "But not from its legacy."'

He didn't know where she was going with this but he did remember the conversation. He answered with a reluctant, 'Yes.'

'I think you're suffering from a legacy too.' She leaned in closer. 'Even though you're now a qualified medical practitioner, the trauma of losing your father at a vulnerable age has blinkered you to the facts. I think you've made a massive non-scientific leap that connects your father's early death with your heart block. The result is an erroneous belief that you'll die young too.'

'It's not unreasonable—'

'It is. The statistics don't support it. Thomas told me you have a two per cent chance of dying from your heart condition. That's way better odds than crossing Piccadilly Circus at rush hour.'

Her words beat hard against his belief that he had a faulty heart just like his father. A belief cemented by the crusty cardiologist who'd said five years ago, 'You can't fight genetics, son.'

'That may be but it doesn't rule out me passing on a faulty heart to a child.'

'And I could just as easily pass on my dyslexia.'

Frustration bit him. 'That's completely different.'

'Yes, it is.'

Her acceptance surprised him and he studied her. She immediately speared him with an intense look that belied her words and made him squirm.

She continued briskly. 'We don't know yet if your condition's inherited or if there are other factors. Want to tell me exactly what happened five years ago?'

He sighed. 'I was working really long hours and training for an ironman competition when I had my first episode of heart block.'

'Athlete's heart syndrome?'

'Yes and no. It's complicated.'

'You need to talk to Thomas and get all the facts, but I know for certain that my dyslexia's inherited. My grandmother and great-grandfather never learned to read. There's a chance a child of ours may have learning challenges.'

A child of ours.

The thought tempted and terrified him in equal measure. He fought back. 'Why don't you get this?' he asked tersely. 'Dyslexia's not a life-threatening condition.'

She folded her arms across her chest. 'It is if it's not treated.'

He snorted. 'No one ever died of dyslexia.'

'People with low self-esteem and no hope die every day,' she said softly, the message in her words sharp and clear.

'We wouldn't allow things to get to that,' he said quickly, stunned by his strong need to protect a child that didn't even exist. 'We'd be on the lookout for any signs of dyslexia. We'd make sure they had access to early intervention. They'd get all the help they needed to thrive.'

'Of course we would,' she said evenly. 'And in exactly the same way, we'd get be on the lookout and get an early diagnosis and intervention for any child of ours who had a cardiac arrhythmia.' A smile wove across her lips. 'I think that's called checkmate.'

'Claire,' he heard himself growl. 'It's not that simple.'

'Alistair,' she sighed. 'It really is. With your pacemaker, your heart's pumping life through you just as it's been doing without error for the last five years, but you're not taking full advantage of what technology's offering you. You can let irrational fear continue to rule your life and keep everyone at arm's length or you can take a chance, embrace love, accept some low-level risk and share your life with me.

'The choice is yours.' Without waiting for him to reply, she rose to her feet and left the room.

Her words filled his head, duelling with his long-held beliefs about his life and the decisions he'd made long ago. Not once in five years had he ever questioned them. Hell, he'd accepted his fate and got on with his life, so why was he even considering what she'd said?

Because you've never been in love before.

How could it be so simple and so bloody complicated? Claire painted a picture of a life with her and children—a life he wanted badly, but either way he risked hurting her.

'Alistair.' Thomas Wolfe strode energetically into the room wearing a grey suit, a crisp white shirt and a pale blue tie. He'd obviously been home and acknowledged the new day with fresh clothes. Only the shadows under his eyes hinted that perhaps all wasn't quite as it appeared. 'Good to see you're awake.'

Alistair grimaced. 'I hear I have a state-of-the-art pacemaker.'

'The silver bullet.' Thomas's eyes lit up. 'It's a great invention. And you can play as much virtual tennis as you want, although at thirty-nine, your shoulder might object.'

Alistair sat up a bit higher. 'You're not that far behind me, old man.'

'Indeed.' Thomas's smile was wry. 'The good news is your cardiac enzymes and ECG are both normal. Your groin will feel a bit sore for a few days and you can't walk until tomorrow, but other than that, you'll be feeling yourself again very soon. No need to let this hiccough slow you down.'

'Hiccough?' He heard the disbelief in his voice.

'It's unfortunate the lead became damaged but you were close to a battery replacement anyway. In a way, you did yourself a favour. This pacemaker is a huge leap forward in the treatment of heart block, and apart from not being able to go scuba-diving or joining the armed forces, your life's your own.'

Was it? Immediately, Claire's accusation that he'd made a massive non-scientific leap about his condition burned him. 'My father died suddenly at forty-seven.'

'Of an MI?'

'I always assumed.'

Thomas checked the tablet computer in his hand. 'Your cholesterol's low, your blood pressure's in the normal range and you don't smoke. All of it puts your risk factor for an MI as very low.' He rubbed his neck. 'Your father could have died of an aneurysm or numerous other things. If it was an MI, then I think you've inherited your mother's heart genes. If you can get hold of your father's medical history, I'd be happy to take a look. Meanwhile, you having problems is not something I'd be betting any money on.'

Again Claire's voice sounded loud and clear in his head.

You can let irrational fear continue to rule your life and keep everyone at arm's length or you can take a chance, embrace love, accept some low-level risk and share your life with me.

A feeling of lightness streaked through him almost raising him off the bed and he stuck out his right hand. 'Thank you, Thomas. You have no idea how much I appreciate your straight-talking.'

'Any time.' Thomas shook his proffered hand. 'I'll see you in the morning before you're discharged but any other questions just call me.' He turned to leave.

'Thomas, before you go, can I ask you a favour?'

One of the hardest things Claire had ever done was walk out of Alistair's hospital room yesterday morning but she'd felt it was her only option. It was that or hit him over the head in frustration. Or beg. She certainly wasn't going to beg. The old Claire may have begged but Alistair had taught her that she didn't need to beg anyone for anything. The lesson wasn't without irony.

Still, she'd been sorely tempted to beg but she'd fought it. In her mind, two things were very clear. The first was that Alistair loved and valued her. The second was that if they were to have any chance at happiness, Alistair had to come to his decision freely and not be cornered or cajoled into committing to her. She also knew that his love for her was a big part of the problem. He didn't want to hurt her and yet by protecting her from life—from his life—he was hurting her ten times over.

'How's the boss?' Andrew asked as they stripped off their surgical gowns.

'If he takes his doctor's advice, he'll be back at work next week.'

'So we can expect him here tomorrow, then.' Andrew winked at her. 'I imagine he's got women lining up to look after him so perhaps he will stay away for the week.'

A bristle ran up Claire's spine. 'The man needs to rest, Andrew.'

He grinned. 'Sure. But hey, what a way to rest.'

Claire hit him with the folder she was holding. 'Go and check your patients in recovery.'

He held up his hands in surrender. 'Yes, Mum. On my way.'

She walked to the doctors' lounge and made herself a late-afternoon snack to keep her energy levels up. She was eating a plate of cheese and biscuits when her phone rang. 'Claire Mitchell.'

'Thomas Wolfe, Claire. As Alistair's indisposed, I was wondering if you could help me out.'

'Ah, sure. Do you have a patient who needs a neuro consult?'

'In a manner of speaking. He's a high-profile private patient and coming here's difficult with the…um…'

'Picket line,' she supplied as her thoughts roved to a possible celebrity child.

'Exactly,' Thomas said firmly. 'They're sending a car. What time suits you?'

'I'll be free in an hour.'

It suddenly occurred to her that perhaps it was a royal child, but as she opened her mouth to ask, Thomas was already saying, 'Excellent. I'll get the porter to buzz you when the driver arrives.'

'Can you give me some de—?' The line went dead. She waited for him to call her back or send a text but nothing came. A skitter of excitement raced through her at the idea of a very top-secret patient. At least it would take her mind off Alistair.

The car wasn't a limousine nor did it have any distinctive crest or signage on it, so Claire wasn't able to glean any clues about the mystery patient from her transport. When she'd quizzed the driver he'd replied that he wasn't at liberty to disclose who'd ordered and paid for the car.

Despite the evening traffic, the drive was thankfully short and soon enough she was standing on the porch of a Victorian town house with a royal-blue door. She rang the recessed brass bell and waited, her curiosity rising and her stomach churning. She probably should have eaten more before coming. She listened intently for footsteps. About thirty seconds later she was still listening. She was about to ring the bell again when the door opened.

Her stomach rolled and she felt her eyes widen. 'Alistair?'

He stood in front of her wearing faded jeans and a button-necked light wool jumper that lit his grey eyes to a burnished pewter. His hair was its usual messy chic and the addition of a five o'clock stubble shadow on his cheeks made him sexier than ever.

'You're not a celebrity child.'

A momentary look of confusion crossed his face. 'Ah, no. Was I supposed to be?'

'Thomas led me to believe…' Actually, Thomas hadn't given any details at all. She'd jumped to those conclusions all on her own. 'Never mind. You've been discharged,' she said, stating the obvious and trying to keep calm when all she wanted to do was hug him tightly. 'You've got your colour back,' she said crisply.

'I feel pretty good. How are you?' A familiar frown creased his brow. 'You look tired.'

She wanted to bask in his concern for her but she'd done that before and it hurt too much. Now, far too much was at stake. 'Yes, well, it's been a big few days.'

He gave her a wan smile. 'It has. Please come in.' He stepped back from the doorway so she could enter but as she passed him she could smell his delicious shower-fresh scent and her heart raced.

She immediately tried to slow it down. The only thing being at his house meant was that he wanted to talk to her. What he planned to say would either cause the crack in her heart to break open for good or it would heal it.

'Go through.' He indicated she walk the length

of the hall and she was very aware of the noise her heels made clicking against his polished floorboards. It echoed into the strained silence.

She entered a large, light-filled space that combined a kitchen, dining area and family room that opened out onto a walled garden. The evening was warm and the sweet perfume of wisteria drifted in through the open French doors. So this was his house? It wasn't the soulless stainless steel and chrome bachelor pad she'd imagined. If anything, it looked of a style and design that was ripe to be filled with the children he was too scared to have.

'I thought we could sit outside?' he suggested politely.

From the moment he'd opened the front door he'd been the perfect host, and if he were going to continue in the same vein when there was so much at stake, she'd go mad. With a shake of her head, she set her handbag down on the dining table next to a vase overflowing with roses, scented lilies, daisies and hypericum berries. They were a beautiful arrangement and most likely get-well-soon flowers, although she wondered at the pink and mauve colour palette for a man.

'I'm a firm believer of ripping a sticking plaster off fast.'

His brows drew down. 'Sorry?'

'Alistair.' His name came out on a sigh. 'I don't want to go through the charade of you offering me a drink and something to eat and then breaking my heart. Just do it now and get it over and done with.'

He looked disconcerted as if they were actors in a play and she'd just gone off-script. He pulled out a chair for her.

'I don't need to sit down if I'm leaving in a minute.'

He rubbed the back of his neck and glanced out towards the garden before looking back at her. 'You're not making this easy.'

She shrugged. 'I didn't think that was my job.'

'No.' He drew in a deep breath. 'I love you, Claire.'

She steeled herself against the thrill that traitorously stole through her. 'I know you do. But for us those three words are hardly reassuring.'

'I'm sorry, Claire…'

Her heart quivered and she found one hand clutching the edge of the table and the other curling around her belly as it lurched and rolled.

'I've been a fool and…'

What? His words began to penetrate her fog of despair. She clawed back her concentration and watched him carefully.

His eyes held sorrow. 'If I had my time over I'd have handled everything differently. I'm standing here before you now begging you to take a chance and risk sharing your life with me.'

For a moment, her astonishment seemed to almost stop time and then her heart leapt at his words—her words. He was saying to her exactly what she'd said to him in the hospital. 'You want to embrace love?'

He reached out his arms. 'I want to embrace love. I want to embrace you and a life together.'

More than anything in the world, she wanted to rush into his arms but something—survival—kept her rooted to the spot. 'And children?' She asked the question softly, barely daring to speak the words out loud for fear they would bring her world crashing down on her again.

'Yes.' He nodded slowly. 'That is, if we're fortunate enough to have them. You're right, Claire. If our kids face challenges, we'll be there with the resources to help.'

Relief and joy—so sweet and strong—surged through her making her sway but still she held herself back from the security of his arms. It was important to her—to them both—that she understood exactly how he'd got to this point. 'What happened to change your mind?'

'You happened.' He stared down at her while his left hand stroked her hair. 'Five years ago, when I collapsed and got the pacemaker, I saw it as a second chance at life. I also believed it came with a very big condition. I couldn't risk having kids and there are very few women out there who don't want the full package of marriage and children. So I focused on work and having fun. When a woman tried to get too close, I broke things off. It was always that easy until I met you.'

'I've always been difficult,' she said, half joking and half serious.

A slow smile broke over his handsome face. 'You're the most wonderfully difficult woman I've ever had the pleasure to know. You're also the only woman I've ever fallen in love with. It threw me so completely that I've behaved abominably.'

The only woman I've ever fallen in love with.

All those beautiful women who'd preceded her and yet it was her—the woman with the learning challenges and a lifetime of idiosyncrasies—she was the one he loved. He wanted to share his life with her come what may. Make a future with her.

Tears pricked the back of her eyes and she raised her hand to his cheek, welcoming the feel of his stubble grazing her palm. 'You were scared.'

'I can't believe how close I got to losing you.' His voice cracked and he cleared his throat. 'Thank you for coming to the hospital and talking sense to me.' His forehead touched hers. 'Thank you for loving me.'

She blinked rapidly as her legs trembled. 'Thank you for loving me.'

His arms wrapped around her, pulling her in so close and tight she could barely breathe. 'Claire?'

'Yes.'

He set her back from him so he could see her face. 'Will you do me the honour of becoming my wife?'

His proposal stunned and thrilled her and she found herself struggling to speak. 'I… That's… I… Yes,' she finally managed to splutter out. 'Yes, yes, yes.'

He grinned at her, his face alight with love. 'Thank goodness for that.' Cupping her cheeks in his hands, he tilted her head back and kissed her with firm, warm and giving lips.

She sighed into him, letting him take her weight and absorbing the solid feel of him against her. His touch and feel radiated love, support and infinite generosity. When he eventually broke the kiss, he said, 'By the way, these flowers are for you. A peace offering for my stupidity. I don't mind if you throw them at me.'

She gave an unsteady laugh as she tried to un-pack everything that was happening—how hope-lessness had been turned on its head to become happiness. 'I can't throw them at you. That would be a waste. They're too beautiful.'

'So are you.' He kissed her again. 'Will you come outside into the garden? Please.'

The entreaty in his voice made it impossible to deny him. 'I think it's probably safe for me to do that now.'

He grinned and gripping her hand he tugged her across the room and out into the garden. A silver champagne bucket stood on a table and protruding from it was the neck of a bottle of champagne with distinctive gold, orange and black foil. A platter of antipasti covered in a fine net cloth sat beside it along with two champagne flutes.

He gave her a sheepish look. 'I'd planned to propose to you out here. I wanted to do my very best to make it as romantic as possible. Make it something you'd remember.'

His love and care circled her in warmth. 'And I went and threw a spanner in the works. Sorry.'

He laughed. 'Hey, I still got the girl so I don't mind at all.' He removed the foil covering on the top of the champagne bottle and then his long, surgical fingers popped the cork. The fizzing liquid quickly filled the fine crystal glasses.

When he'd set the bottle back into the ice bucket, she stepped into his arms and ran her hands through his hair. 'You've got more than just me.'

He gazed down at her. 'In-laws, you mean?

My mother's keen to meet you, and we can take a trip to—'

She pressed her fingers to his lips as she shook her head. 'I don't mean my family. I mean our family.'

He looked increasingly bewildered so she took pity on him. 'It turns out I didn't have gastro.'

His eyes widened into silver moons. 'You're pregnant?' Hope and awe tumbled from his whispered words.

'Six weeks.' She couldn't stop a broad smile despite knowing she needed to urge caution. 'It's still early days and you know that anything could hap—' She gave a squeal of surprise as her feet suddenly left the ground.

Alistair spun her around and around, his face alight with sheer delight. 'You're amazing. This is amazing.'

She threw back her head and laughed, revelling in more joy than she'd ever known. The circular motion eventually caught up with her and she suddenly gripped his shoulders. 'Feeling sick.'

He stopped abruptly and set her down on the chair. 'Sorry. Drink this.' He picked up the champagne and then laughed and put it down again. 'I'll get you something else.'

When he returned a short moment later the world had stilled on its axis and she was feeling a little better. She accepted the glass of apple juice he'd poured into a champagne glass.

Squatting by her side, he picked up his champagne flute. 'To my darling Claire, for opening my eyes and giving me back my life.'

She leaned in and kissed him, her heart so full it threatened to burst in her chest. 'To my darling Alistair, for opening my eyes so I can appreciate my strengths and skills.'

'You're most welcome.' He grinned up at her. 'Someone wise once told me that we're good for each other.'

'And don't you forget it. I love you, Alistair North.'

'I love you too, Claire Mitchell. Here's to a life lived to the full. To facing challenges head-on and to the joy of children.'

She thought about what they'd taught each other. 'To enough routine to make life enjoyable and enough spontaneity to keep it fun.'

They raised their glasses and clinked. 'To the future.'

And then he kissed her and she knew she was home.

EPILOGUE

'Do you think international travel with children comes under the heading of spontaneity and fun?' Alistair asked with a wry smile as he tramped along a wide, golden sand beach with a baby carrier on his back.

Claire laughed as she adjusted the baby carrier on her own back. 'Nothing about travelling with babies and all of their associated gear can be called spontaneous.'

'Their creation, however, was both spontaneous and fun,' Alistair teased as he slid his hand into hers and squeezed it.

'It was.' She leaned in and kissed him on the cheek. She was more in love with him now than on the day she'd said, 'I do,' in the beautiful stained-glass chapel at the castle and she was absolutely stunned that it was even possible. 'Bringing the twins to my homeland is fun.'

The twins—a boy and a girl now eleven months old—squealed in delight. Thrashing their arms wildly, they touched hands now that their parents were walking close enough so they could reach each other from their carriers.

Claire breathed in the fresh, salty air and felt peace invade her bones. She enjoyed London but she loved Australia and its wide-open spaces more. She couldn't quite believe she—*they*—were here in Queensland. The last nineteen months had been momentous. Two weeks after Alistair had proposed, he'd accompanied her to the routine pregnancy ultrasound. As she lay on the table with her hand encased in Alistair's, excitement on hearing the baby's heartbeat had turned from joy to shock and back to joy again when they'd heard two heartbeats.

'Twins? But how?' she'd asked inanely.

Alistair had laughed. 'Any twins in your family?'

'Dad has twin brothers.'

'There you go,' he'd said, kissing her on the forehead. 'Now this is the sort of inherited condition I can get behind.'

Being pregnant and studying for her exams had been tough but with her study regime and Alistair's help—both practical and emotional—she'd passed. The good news had arrived just before she'd gone into labour. A paediatrician had been on hand at the birth to check for any cardiac irregularities but both children were declared to have healthy hearts. Their six-month check-ups had all been normal and they were kicking goals on all their developmental milestones, although Claire noticed Emily did things just that little bit earlier than Noah. It was typical girl power.

Parenthood had brought with it both joy and delight along with exhaustion, but she and Alistair were used to functioning on limited sleep courtesy of years of working in hospitals. It didn't faze them too much. They'd become experts at walking the floor, bouncing the pram and driving around London in the wee small hours, all sure-fire ways to get unsettled babies back to sleep. The biggest surprise—and the most appreciated—had been Alistair's decision to cut back his work hours so he could be around more for hands-on help. Claire, loving motherhood but missing work, took up the two days a week that Alistair had dropped. It was a perfect solution. Just recently, with the twins close to their first birthday, they felt they'd found their groove and had decided to bring them out to Australia to meet her parents as well as taking a well-earned beach holiday.

At the prospect of the twenty-four-hour journey, Alistair had said, 'We're either brave or stupid.'

'We're both,' she'd said, kissing him with gratitude. 'And I love you for it.'

A pacific gull and a cormorant swooped over the gently breaking waves and then dived, probably having just spotted a school of fish and dinner. The sun, now a vivid orange ball of fire, dropped low to the horizon, shooting out fingers of red and yellow flames that lit up the scudding clouds. Claire felt the chill in the breeze for the first time.

'We should probably take them home.'

'Dinner, bath, bed?'

'For us or them?' she teased.

His eyes darkened just the way she liked. 'Twins first and then us.'

'I'll hold you to that.' They turned around and walked back towards the beach access track. Not able to hold back her sigh, she said, 'I can't believe we've only got one day of our holiday left.'

'What if we stayed?'

She laughed and gave him a gentle elbow in the ribs. 'You're just procrastinating because you don't want to face the flight back to London.'

'Well, there is that,' he said with a grin, but then his expression sobered. 'I'm serious, Claire. What if we stayed and worked in Australia? I enjoyed my time in Sydney as a registrar so I know what I'm in for. I've loved this holiday and I love this country. Your mother's besotted by the twins—'

'There's not a big call for neurosurgeons in

Gundiwindi,' she said, thinking of her dusty hometown.

'True, but there is in Brisbane. The city's only a few hours' drive away for your parents, which is a lot closer than London. Plus, your dad's talking about retiring closer to the coast.'

'Is he?'

'He told me they'd been looking at properties in the hinterland.'

Her mother had mentioned something in passing along those lines but she hadn't thought anything of it because she couldn't imagine her father ever leaving Gundiwindi. The idea of having her parents closer for support was very tempting, as was the opportunity for the twins to grow up with grandparents. 'But what about your mother?' she asked, trying to be fair. 'If we stay here, then she misses out.'

'You know as well as I do Mother's not really a natural at being an extra-pair-of-hands type of a grandmother. She prefers children when they're older. We'll Skype her each week and buy a big house with a large guest room and an en-suite. She can fly out anytime she wants to visit. But I can pretty much guarantee she won't do that until they're at school.'

Anticipation and excitement started to bubble in her veins. She stopped walking and turned to face him. 'You've really thought about this, haven't you?'

'I have.'

'What about our friends and colleagues? The castle? Won't you miss the old girl?'

'Paddington's always going to have a place in my heart, because it's where I met you. But times change and we need to change with them.'

She'd never asked him to consider moving to Australia because they'd met in London. 'You'd really do this for me?'

'It's not a hardship, Claire. Yesterday, when you were at the beach with your parents, I made enquiries at Brisbane's public and private hospitals.' He stroked her face. 'Would you like to go into private practice with me in Brisbane, Ms Mitchell?'

Marvelling at how lucky she was to have him in her life, she didn't have to think twice. 'Yes, please.' Throwing her arms around her neck, she kissed him, welcoming the future and all it had to offer.

* * * * *